HEI

CW00811937

INTRUDER IN PARADISE

Selena Brent had been Miss Hallows' companion for two years, and she treasured Cloudhallows as though it belonged to her. Unfortunately, when Miss Hallows died, it was beyond Selena's pocket, and she could only wonder who would buy the house. She was convinced it would be a brash, insensitive type who would want the lovely old building modernised and dragged into the twentieth-century. But that was just the first wrong conclusion she was to make about Mark Denning . . .

Books by Stella Kent
in the Linford Romance Library:

THE CAUTIOUS HEART
PROUD CITADEL
CLAUDIA ON THE WING
PERILOUS MASQUERADE
THE WAYWARD HEART

STELLA KENT

INTRUDER IN PARADISE

Complete and Unabridged

LINFORD
Leicester

First published in Great Britain in 1985

First Linford Edition
published 2010

British Library CIP Data

Kent, Stella, *1927* – .
  Intruder in paradise. - -
  (Linford romance library)
  1. Love stories.
  2. Large type books.
  I. Title II. Series
  823.9'14–dc22

  ISBN 978–1–44480–491–1

Published by
F. A. Thorpe (Publishing)
Anstey, Leicestershire

Set by Words & Graphics Ltd.
Anstey, Leicestershire
Printed and bound in Great Britain by
T. J. International Ltd., Padstow, Cornwall

This book is printed on acid-free paper

1

'I'm sorry, Selena,' the estate agent said again. 'I know getting the house meant a lot to you.'

Selena Brent tried for a smile. 'It was never more than a dream. I had ideas above my station!'

'Nonsense.' John Farmer came round from behind his desk and patted her slim shoulder awkwardly. 'You would have been a perfect owner and Miss Hallows would have loved you to have the place. But this is an excellent offer, far higher than we anticipated. I have to advise the executors to accept it.'

'But Cloudhallows was to be sold by auction,' Selena protested forlornly, 'and it's still ten days away.'

'"Unless previously sold",' Farmer quoted. 'It was stated in the brochure. In fact, I've had two other offers, but they were little over the reserve.'

'You didn't ask me how high *I* could go.'

'That's not really how it's done, my dear. However, I was going to tip you the wink about the position. Then, when this bid came in, I thought I would ask you to come over for a chat. It was the least I could do. You're still living at Cloudhallows and I know how you feel about the place.'

Selena looked down at the toes of her shoes, a little muddy from her walk over the fields. John Farmer had his business in Tivenham, the nearest small town, ten miles away, but his home was in Fairbridge, only half-a-mile from Cloudhallows.

Selena had known him vaguely all her life. He had been an acquaintance of her father's when he had been a schoolmaster in Tivenham, and he had been kind and helpful to her when she had sold the family house on her father's death.

'I know how much your father's house fetched,' he went on now, 'and I don't suppose there was a great deal of cash.'

'I could have borrowed more.'

'I don't know about that. You haven't a real job, have you? Just a sort of companion to old Miss Hallows, and that's gone now.' He cleared his throat. 'What happened to that husband of yours?'

A flush coloured Selena's ivory skin. Quite a beauty, Farmer thought. She took after her long-dead mother there, with her copper-coloured hair and wide-set hazel-green eyes. What man in his right mind would have let her get away — and a large sum of money with her, his hard business head added.

'Michael and I have been divorced for nearly two years,' Selena said shortly. 'I was married at eighteen, and had never trained for anything. I don't know what I shall do now.'

'I remember — your father was very upset. He'd set his heart on you going to University. I never understood why you sold your own home.'

'I didn't want to stay there.' She couldn't bring herself to elaborate on the misery of her last twelve months in the house where she had crept back after the collapse of her marriage, to nurse her father in his final illness.

★   ★   ★

She had sold the house, and looking round for a breathing space, she had met Miss Rose Hallows, kind, intelligent and witty, and looking for a young companion, and she had gone to live at enchanting old Cloudhallows.

'Of course, you'll know that young Stephen Tremar has expressed an interest in the property,' said John Farmer. 'Hasn't got much capital yet, but, as a vet, his future is secure.' He shot Selena a glance. 'No chance of — er — a merger of any sort, I suppose?'

Selena laughed. 'No! No chance.'

'Not a case of once bitten, twice shy, or any nonsense like that, I hope.

Tremar's a very good chap. Thoroughly reliable. Different kettle of fish altogether from that other young man.'

'It's nothing like that.' Selena sipped her sherry. There was no need for John Farmer to point out the difference between Stephen Tremar and Michael. It formed the basis of her affection for Stephen. But, despite his urging to turn it into something deeper, friendship was all she was ready for.

'Can you tell me how much the bid for Cloudhallows is?' she asked. 'So that I know it's quite beyond me.'

Farmer hesitated for a moment then named a figure which seemed to Selena highly inflated.

Her last hope died. 'But that's ridiculous! The house needs loads doing to it, and it's quite off the beaten track. Has this man actually seen it? Has he had his own survey done?'

'Now, Selena, you know I can't go into any details. As far as I'm aware, he's only seen the brochure. But Cloudhallows has potential — perhaps he plans to extend it. And the new spur to the trunk road will be through in a couple of years — '

'Extend Cloudhallows!' Selena exploded. 'What sort of a Philistine is he? It's a perfect sixteenth-century house. He would never get permission. And as for a motor-way roaring alongside it, Stephen and I are fighting that.'

'Maybe he doesn't intend anything of the sort. I don't know. I've only been in contact with his solicitor. Very likely he'll love it — as you do — just as it is. As for the new road, despite Tremar's ferocity, it is not a motorway, and its route shouldn't disturb Cloudhallows in any way. If Tremar has been putting it about to the contrary,' he added severely, 'it could account for the relatively little interest in the property.'

The spirit had gone out of Selena. 'What is he like, this private buyer?'

'I haven't met him, but he seems a decisive character. He knows what he wants.'

Selena grimaced. 'Then I'd better

pack my things and be ready to move out.'

She shook hands with the estate agent and he showed her to the front door. She turned the collar of her tweed coat up against the chill February air and stuck her hands in her pockets.

★　★　★

It was no great tragedy, she reminded herself as she crossed the lane in front of John Farmer's gate and climbed the stile to the fields beyond which lay Cloudhallows. She should be ashamed of her feelings of self-pity. With a decent sum of money in her account she could pick and choose a small country property. But not Cloudhallows.

She reached the crest of the hill, from where she could see the lovely old house rooted in its hollow, its lichened grey roof half-hidden by trees, a trickle of smoke trailing from one of its tall chimneys. A sudden cold wind made her eyes water and she set off at a jog over the ice-hard ruts of the hillside.

She climbed over the stile at the bottom and walked the short distance down the lane to Cloudhallows. The last rays of the winter sun glinted on the mullioned windows and the rosy brick traversed by oak beams that had faded to a pale lavender. It was an enchanted world, detached from modern life. A time-warp, Selena thought as she opened the gate.

She opened the heavy studded door and stepped straight into the big square hall. She poked at the ashy pile of logs in the enormous fireplace she could have stood upright in, and added another couple to the heap. She drew the curtains at the downstairs windows and, going to the kitchen, made herself a tray of tea which she carried into Miss Hallows' pretty little sitting room. The fireplace here had been much reduced to take a small coal-burning grate and Selena drew her armchair close to it. Afterwards, she would think about packing. Perhaps it was a good thing.

Two years was long enough for a resilient young woman to reside in a backwater, licking her wounds.

'How your husband must have hurt you,' Miss Hallows had said to her more than once.

But he hadn't meant to, Selena's heart had protested. Michael never hurt people intentionally. It was just that he was single-minded, and anyone who got in his way or couldn't keep up with his wild schemes simply fell by the wayside.

★ ★ ★

She had met him when she was just eighteen and he eight years older. Three months later they had been married. His blue-eyed, black-haired good looks and his effervescent personality had charmed her as they charmed almost everyone, with the notable exception of her father. He wouldn't have approved of anyone who took his unpaid housekeeper away from him and, in any case, he distrusted charm.

After four years, she had returned home, unable to stand Michael's hare-brained schemes, the lies and the fraud, any longer.

It was small wonder that, after her father had died, she had been so happy in Miss Hallows' kindly, humorous company. But there must be no more living in the past. She would start getting her things together right away. She picked up the tea-tray and had started for the door when the phone bell rang.

She put down the tray again and picked up the phone from the bureau.

'Selena?' It was Stephen Tremar's firm, quiet voice. 'What happened to you? I thought you were coming over for tea this afternoon.'

'Oh, Stephen, I'm dreadfully sorry. I completely forgot.'

'Think nothing of it. It was just that Chrissie was a bit anxious. Apparently she baked some sort of special cake and she wondered where you had got to.'

'I'm sorry,' Selena said again. She

rather doubted that the special cake had been solely for her benefit and it was certainly nothing new to be a source of irritation to Stephen's doting cousin. 'Please apologise to Chris for me.'

'Is anything the matter?'

'No, nothing really. Well, John Farmer asked me to go to his house this afternoon. He told me that he had had a good bid for Cloudhallows from a private buyer and the executors are accepting it. The house is being withdrawn from sale.'

There was a lengthy silence at the other end of the line, then Stephen said, 'I'm sorry.'

'So am I. Although I thought it would probably go over what I could pay, I still went on hoping.'

'I could have lent you money towards it. Not a great deal, but — '

'Thank you, Stephen. That's very generous, but I couldn't possibly take it. I couldn't afford to pay off a mortgage and private loans. This offer was for far more than I could raise.'

'Who's the buyer? Is he local?' asked Stephen.

'I don't know. I don't think so. It isn't anyone I showed over the house. Probably some high-flying executive with a pack of spoilt children.'

* * *

There was a rather dispirited pause, then Stephen said, 'I hope we can rely on his support over the road protest. It's really only the owner of Cloud-hallows who has any chance of influencing the tribunal.'

'I somehow feel this man won't object to the road a bit.'

'I hope you're wrong. A road alongside Cloudhallows would be an outrage. Oh, Selena, I wish you were going to be living there.'

'So do I. But, really, I suppose it was a bit ridiculous. What would I want with six bedrooms?'

'If you were thinking of re-marry-ing — ' His words hung in the air.

'I was just going to start packing,' Selena said quickly.

'It's not that urgent, is it?' He sounded forlorn. 'I can't bear to think of you going away.'

The long pent-up tears roughened her voice. 'I shall hate leaving.'

'Shall I come over?'

She hesitated. 'No, Stephen. I think I want to be on my own.'

'I don't like to think of you alone there. It's very secluded.'

'I've been alone here for two months now.'

'Does Mrs. Hardy still come in?'

'Only for a couple of hours in the mornings.'

'What about the gardener?'

'Jordan? He was laid off after he got the garden into shape for prospective buyers. I don't know whether the new owner will want to re-engage him. Good gardeners are hard to find.'

'What about you? What will you do?'

'Unfortunately, I'm not so well-qualified as Jordan. I'll have to look around.'

'You could do a few hours for me.'

'Oh, Stephen, what would Chris have to say to that? She's more than capable of keeping your appointments and helping in the surgery.'

Stephen sighed. His cousin's devotion sometimes weighed heavily on him. 'Well — if you're sure you'll be all right alone — '

'I'm quite sure, thank you, Stephen. I'll ring you tomorrow.'

She put down the phone and carried her tray through to the kitchen. There she washed her dishes and tidied the kitchen ready for Mrs. Hardy's arrival in the morning.

The elderly daily had, for many years, prepared the mid-day meal, but Selena had discontinued this after the old lady's death, just keeping her on for a couple of hours' cleaning in the mornings and paying her out of her own pocket.

She knew Mrs. Hardy was anxious to keep her job, and she intended to recommend her, although somehow she couldn't see this new broom wanting to take over Miss Hallows' employees.

★ ★ ★

She locked the outer doors before going upstairs to her room. It was not the largest she could have chosen, but she had loved it on sight, with its eccentrically sloping, polished wood floor and its cream-washed walls segmented by oak beams. The curtains and covers were flower-sprigged on a soft green background. The room was at the back of the house and looked out over the boughs of an apple tree.

Selena began to collect her things together in a desultory way. She hadn't brought much from her father's house, just her books, some trinkets and ornaments of her mother's, and a few photographs.

One thing she mustn't forget was the book she had begun on the history of Cloudhallows.

She drifted into the small library. The

books and papers that she had been working on the evening, two months ago, when Miss Hallows had been suddenly taken ill were on the desk where she had left them, the place markers still in position. Sitting at the desk, she took her notes from the drawer and began to look through them.

The idea of a history of the house and its inhabitants had begun as a diversion for the old lady whose lively mind was increasingly thwarted by her failing body. At first Selena had listened with interest to her memories of life at Cloudhallows, in the village, and the 'big' houses round about in the early years of the century. Then, guided by Miss Hallows, she had searched out older records, journals and accounts in the largely unclassified library.

Gradually, what had been a means of interesting the old lady and passing her own free time, began to take hold of her as she searched out and photocopied archives from the local library, the county records office, and parish registers.

Who would be interested now in the people who had lived and died in the house throughout the centuries? she wondered. The new owner? There was something about his grabbing of the place, sight unseen, that suggested otherwise. She returned the papers to the drawer and tidied the stacked books.

It was time to move on, she reminded herself again. Where was the adventurous spirit that had filled her at eighteen when she had taken her bold leap with Michael so soon after meeting him? Had it been eroded by the years of his betrayal of her trust? Now she was ready to begin again. A new job, a new home, perhaps a holiday. She had always enjoyed travel. And romance?

Her mind shied away. She missed Michael's love-making with an intensity that, in the early days of their separation, had almost consumed her.

She had cried herself to sleep many times in her longing to be one with him again.

She got to her feet in a swift movement. But no, not romance just yet. And a casual affair without an emotional commitment, she knew was not for her.

So in the meantime? 'In the meantime,' she resolved as she headed for the staircase, 'we pack.'

* * *

Selena woke the next morning to find pale golden sunshine filtering through the curtains at her casement window. The air was still chill, however, and she snuggled beneath the covers for a few minutes before dashing for the bathroom. As the water filled the tub, she wondered whether the new owner had read the brochure carefully enough to realise that Cloudhallows only possessed one bathroom, and that the hot water supply was by no means reliable.

The fact that a blackbird sang deliciously in the tree beneath the window would, she felt, be little compensation.

But today the cistern was behaving itself and her bath was agreeably hot. When she had finished, she pulled on a sweater and slacks, brushed her bright hair, and went downstairs to the kitchen.

She loved the big, welcoming room with its warm, red tiles, the oak dresser shining with blue and white china, and the cheering stove glowing in the inglenook.

She checked the hall for non-existent post while she waited for the kettle to boil, then sat down with her breakfast. From the table she could see into the back garden, enclosed by a wall of ancient, uneven bricks. There was little to see now, just clusters of snowdrops and crocuses peeping out of the black earth, but soon, she knew, it would be alive with colour and scent. Narcissus and pansies, Sweet William and stock, sweet-smelling lavender and wallflowers, and the massed roses of June.

★   ★   ★

Selena was washing up her dishes when she heard Mrs. Hardy removing her boots in the back porch. As was her habit, she had commenced her conversation before she was in earshot, and Selena had the feeling that she had come in halfway.

'If you're going to keep a nasty animal like that you should keep it chained up, I told him. Or at least keep your gate shut and not have it dashing out snapping and snarling at innocent passers-by, I told him.'

She came through the open kitchen door, tying an apron round her plump middle, cheeks rosy from the combination of cold and righteous indignation.

'The Reardons?' Selena sympathised.

'Who else? If it's not the dog, it's them kids.'

'Have a cup of tea before you start.'

'I won't say no.' She sat down, pushed her feet into battered working shoes, and accepted the proffered cup. 'Not that it's the poor little devils' fault,' she conceded, her better nature coming to the fore. 'Not properly brought up, they aren't. Anyway, love, what are you going to be doing today?'

'I'm going into the village this morning and, after lunch, I thought I would go to Tivenham.' Selena hesitated to tell Mrs. Hardy she was going to discuss with John Farmer her position at Cloudhallows. But she was going to have to know sooner or later that the house was sold and her days probably numbered. There was no point in dragging it out. 'The house has been bought, Mrs. Hardy.'

'Bought?' was the horrified response. 'But what about the auction?'

'A private buyer made a very good bid and the executors are going to accept it.'

'Who was it, do you know? Was it the

Scottish couple with the little girl? They seemed nice.'

Selena smiled. 'No. Mr. Farmer didn't seem to think the buyer had seen the house.'

'Fancy buying a house you hadn't seen.' Mrs. Hardy brooded for a moment, then said, 'Well, I'll be getting my cards soon, I expect.'

'I'll have to move out myself. That's what I'm going to see Mr. Farmer about. I'll put in a word for you, of course, but I don't know if it will carry much weight.'

* * *

The older woman got slowly to her feet and rinsed her cup at the sink. 'It won't be the same though. Twenty-seven years I was with Miss Hallows, and she was the sweetest lady in the world.'

'I know.' Selena patted Mrs. Hardy's shoulder. 'I'm sorry. It must be very hard for you. If there's anything I can do?'

'Thank you, dear. You're a kind girl and you made Miss Hallows very happy. But it's no use moping. Everything has to come to an end. Well, I'd best give everywhere a thorough going-over. Make a good impression!'

Cheered by the thought of action, she began to pull out her cleaning materials from the cupboard beneath the sink, and Selena retreated. She had intended simply to put on her anorak to visit Stephen, but it occurred to her that she had worn nothing except practical, unglamorous sweaters, skirts and slacks for months. If she was to make any sort of impression on her re-entry into the world, it might be as well to start rehearsing.

She went up to her room and, rummaging around at the back of her wardrobe, came up with her black jumpsuit. She teamed it with soft black leather boots and tied a green silk scarf at her throat.

Returning downstairs, Mrs. Hardy spotted her crossing the hall.

23

'Ooh, you look lovely, dear. Going to see Mr. Tremar, are you?'

Selena grimaced at her. 'I'm going to the village.'

'But you'll pop in to see him, won't you? It'll cheer him up. A nice change from having to look at that bun-faced cousin of his all day.'

Selena frowned reprovingly although she was inclined to agree that there was something bun-like about Chrissie's face, and a rather indigestible bun at that.

She didn't like to be uncharitable, but Chrissie had never attempted to disguise her dislike for her. What seemed to be rudeness was partly, she knew, a gauche defensiveness and fear of losing Stephen to Selena, but it didn't make her company any more agreeable.

She walked down the short stretch of lane and turned into the rather wider road that led to the village. Right on the corner stood the big shabby house that was always known as the Corner

House. Here Stephen and Chris had been born within a year of each other and brought up together, the only children of two brothers. When the last of their parents had died, while Stephen was away at veterinary college, Chris had rented out the family house, bought a small, neat house in the centre of the village, and waited to keep house for him on his return.

At present the Corner House was occupied by the large Reardon clan.

★   ★   ★

The pretty cottages in the main street of the village straggled out to meet Selena. She passed the tiny Post Office and general store and rounded the corner to a village green, flanked by houses on three sides. A dazzling brass plate announced the Tremars' house.

She skirted the immaculately-kept front garden and opened a side gate that led to a yard bounded by kennels and dog runs. Chris' hobby was breeding spaniels and she occasionally boarded a few animals. The state of the backyard was in marked contrast to the bandbox neatness of the front.

Chrissie Tremar was in the corner of the yard, and looked round as Selena appeared. Her sturdy figure was clad in an ancient tweed skirt, a quilted nylon waistcoat over a sweater, and Wellington boots. Her cheeks were reddened by the wind and her rust-coloured hair had blown into a bush. Her gooseberry-green eyes registered Selena's appearance with disapproval, and she said, 'Good heavens, you're dressed to kill!'

'Yes, idiotic, isn't it?' Selena agreed. 'I suddenly felt like a change of image. I'm practising for when I rejoin the outside world.'

'What do you mean? Oh, for when you leave Cloudhallows? Stephen said you would be going.'

Selena leant over the railing of a pen and pulled at the feathery ears of a spaniel puppy. 'I don't have any choice.'

'Not really your sort of place,

anyway, is it? You must have been bored stiff.'

'No, I loved it.' Selena tickled the pup's tummy and sent it into ecstasies. Its reaction seemed to irritate Chris.

'I can understand you would want to hide yourself away for a bit after your husband left you, but I should have thought you'd have had enough of rural peace by now.'

★ ★ ★

Selena had no intention of rising to the bait and setting the record straight on her marriage break-up. If Chris derived some sort of consolation from her version of events, she was welcome to it.

Instead she smiled and asked, 'Is Stephen in?'

Chris' eyes flew to the house and then to the garage. 'I think he went out.'

'His car is there.'

At that moment Stephen appeared at the kitchen door. His face lit up when he saw Selena.

27

He was wearing one of the dazzling white coats, quite impractical for a country vet, with which Chrissie kept him constantly supplied.

Selena grinned. 'Hello, Doctor Kildare.'

He laughed. 'You're in better spirits this morning. I thought you sounded a bit down last night.'

She gestured at her outfit. 'I decided it was time to put out more flags.'

'Devastating!' He put an arm around her shoulders. 'Come inside, there's coffee on.'

Selena let herself be led inside, conscious of Chrissie's eyes boring into her back. She perched on a stool in the Tremars' kitchen.

'Aren't you having a surgery this morning?'

'Not really. Old Miss Crowther brought Fred in again. That cat's a complete hypochondriac. He pays for my petrol single-pawed.' He handed Selena her coffee. 'Have you heard anything further about the sale?'

'No, I'm going to Tivenham after lunch. I thought I'd look in on John Farmer to find out when I have to leave.'

'It'll be grim here without you. I can't tell you what a difference you've made.'

'I'm not looking forward to going.'

★   ★   ★

He moved to the window where he could see Chrissie plodding around the yard. 'I wish I could get away myself.'

'You, Stephen? But you've lived here all your life.'

'All the more reason for a change of scene.' He paused. 'I'm trapped, you know, Selena.'

Embarrassed, she didn't answer.

'Oh, it's not only Chrissie,' he went on. 'It's this house as well. It's too small to do anything with and the neighbours naturally complain if we have too many animals. Chris has set her heart on a sort of animal sanctuary, and expanding

29

the dog breeding, but it's out of the question here.'

'Cloudhallows wouldn't have been very suitable for that. There isn't enough land.'

'I know. I couldn't have afforded it, anyway. I can't buy anything else while I'm lumbered with the old house and I'll never get the Reardons out, not with that crowd of kids. I'll never know why Chris rented it while I was away. It would have been ideal for her purpose.'

Selena had wondered this herself and the only solution she could come up with was that Chrissie, perhaps unconsciously, had wanted to sever the tie with the family house where she and Stephen had been brought up as cousins, almost as brother and sister, and start afresh in something more resembling a marital home. But it was a theory that would have scared the wits out of Stephen and she was glad to be saved answering by the entrance of Chris.

She shucked off her boots by the door, washed her hands at the sink, and poured herself a cup of coffee.

She looked anxiously at Stephen's gloomy face. 'What's the matter?'

'I was wondering what the new people at Cloudhallows will be like.'

'They'll probably be very nice.' It was obvious that, to Chrissie, anything would be an improvement. 'We could do with some fresh faces in the village. Do you know anything about them, Selena?'

'Not a thing, only that John Farmer said he was a decisive character who knew what he wanted.'

'There you are then, Stephen! He could be a valuable ally over the protest. He may have useful connections.' She turned back to Selena. 'Do you think we'll be able to involve him?'

'How would I know? He'd probably like a four-lane highway up to the front door.' Occasionally the Tremars' obsession over the proposed new road got on

Selena's nerves. She couldn't see that it would greatly interfere with Cloud-hallows, and even less with the Corner House, but to voice such an opinion invariably brought a lecture down on her head.

'Stephen will be able to talk him round,' Chris said confidently. She went to the pantry and began to unload a solid-looking cake from a tin. 'Have some cake, Selena. I made it for your tea yesterday.'

'Oh, Chrissie, I'm sorry! I meant to apologise for not coming. I was feeling a bit upset. The cake looks absolutely delicious, but I'm afraid I couldn't manage any.'

'I suppose you have to watch your figure,' Chris said smugly, cutting two large wedges of cake.

'Actually, I'm very lucky. I can eat like a horse. But I'd better be off. I have a couple of calls to make and, as I said, I want to go to Tivenham this afternoon.'

'Yes, they'll be wanting you out as

soon as possible, I expect.' Chris' gift for the inelegant phrase had not deserted her.

'More than likely. And I want to know what's going to happen to Miss Hallows' furniture. If it's still going to auction, there are one or two things I would like.'

★   ★   ★

She said her goodbyes and left, Stephen gazing after her from the door and looking rather like one of Chrissie's spaniels.

She made her calls in the village, then retraced her footsteps to Cloudhallows.

Mrs. Hardy had left in her absence. Selena cooked herself some lunch, washed her dishes, and went outside to her car.

There was no garage at Cloudhallows and cars were housed in a doorless old stone barn near the house. Selena looked at her spanking new sports car, her sole buy from her inheritance, with more than her usual glow of pride. It suited her determined, new image. 'I'll have rally stripes put on!' she decided as she swung through the gap that had been left in the hedge into the lane.

The ten miles drive to Tivenham, through winding country lanes, was a pleasant one for the driver not in a hurry. Selena made her way to John Farmer's office, which fronted the square, next door to a big seventeenth-century coaching inn. There was no one else in the waiting-room and Mr. Farmer's secretary sent Selena straight in.

The estate agent looked as though he had lunched well in the neighbouring establishment. He heaved his portly frame to his feet when Selena came in. 'Hello, my dear. It's a pleasure to see you again so soon. Take a seat. How can I help you?'

★ ★ ★

Selena sat down. 'I'm sorry to bother you again so soon, but I didn't ascertain yesterday when I had to be out of Cloudhallows. I suppose I really shouldn't be there at all.'

'I was going to get in touch with you about that. I talked to the buyer this morning and told him of your position and he said that there was no hurry at all over your leaving. In fact, he would prefer someone to be there.'

'Oh, that's good. I can take my time while I decide what to do. Do you know when he intends to move in?'

'Well, I don't know that he does. As far as I can make out he just intends to use it for weekend guests. What he called hospitality for business clients. Some sort of tax dodge, I shouldn't wonder.'

Selena wrinkled her nose. 'I don't like the sound of that. I've got to get out of the habit of thinking it's anything to do with me, but it doesn't seem the right thing for Cloudhallows.'

'No, I know what you mean. Cloudhallows is a home. But, of course, it's near good fishing and an excellent golf course, and, when the new road goes past — '

'It will be a regular little country club,' she finished.

'Well, as you say, Selena, it's not our business. The legatee couldn't care less what happens to it as long as he gets his money.'

'What about the furniture? That was the other thing I wanted to ask you about. Will it still go to auction?'

'I mentioned that to the buyer. Obviously, he wants to see it. He'll make an offer for the estate for anything he wants, and the rest will be auctioned later.'

'There are one or two things I particularly like. I'd like to bid for them.'

'Well, maybe the two of you can come to some agreement. I don't suppose he'll want to keep everything.'

'No, his taste probably runs to neon-lit cocktail bars,' Selena said unreasonably. 'Business hospitality, indeed!' She held out her hand. 'Goodbye, and thank you, Mr. Farmer.'

John Farmer got to his feet and clasped her hand. 'Goodbye, Selena. Be sure to let me know your plans.'

★   ★   ★

Selena went out into the sunlit square. There was nothing pressing to take her back to Fairbridge, so she spent some time strolling around the attractive old town, many of whose shops and houses were as old as Cloudhallows. She explored the maze of narrow lanes beneath the jettied overhang of the houses, finally emerging at the Tudor Rose, the tea-shop where she had first met Miss Hallows.

It was in a small, half-timbered house directly across the square from the estate agents. Selena ordered tea and buttered scones, and recalled the day, two years ago, when she had sat in the same window seat.

She had just left the estate agent's office after finalising the details of the sale of her father's house and was, she supposed, gazing across at the office.

A quiet voice near to her had said, 'It's heartbreaking, isn't it? Selling the house one loves.'

Selena had jumped. She had been lost in a reverie, but now, looking round, she saw an old lady sitting straight-backed at the corner table. A slender old lady looking frail, yet at the same time full of life, wearing a heather-coloured tweed coat and with soft white curls showing beneath a wine-coloured velvet hat.

'Forgive me. I'm so sorry to have intruded,' the woman said, 'but John Farmer told me a little of your circumstances. You had the appointment following mine.'

'You're selling your house?' Selena tried to show an interest she didn't feel, and was distressed to see the woman turn her head away to hide her tears.

'I can't see any alternative,' she had murmured. And somehow the whole story had come out.

Afterwards, Miss Hallows had told Selena that never before had she bared her soul in such a way to a complete stranger, but something about Selena had appealed to her. She'd joined her at her table, and soon Selena was hearing the story of Cloudhallows, where Miss Hallows had lived all her life and where her family had lived for an unbroken four hundred years. Now there was no one left except a second cousin only ten years younger than Miss Hallows herself who certainly didn't want the place, and she could no longer manage alone.

Selena was temporarily homeless. On an impulse she had offered to stay with Miss Hallows, on a month's mutual trial, while she considered what to do with her life.

It had lasted for two happy years. Selena had loved Cloudhallows on sight, and she liked the village of Fairbridge. She had met Stephen who had become a very pleasant companion, and gradually the pain of her broken marriage and her father's wretched last year of life had been soothed in the quiet day-to-day routine.

★   ★   ★

Selena sighed and finished her tea. It was time to be leaving if she was to get back to Fairbridge before dark. She went to her car and started on her return journey. How many times in the past twenty-four hours had she vowed to slough off the past and think of the future? Yet, as she turned up the lane from the Corner House towards Cloud-hallows, her mind was far away, lost in memories.

She spun the wheel to swing into the opening just beyond the house and almost collided with a large car parked out of sight, completely blocking the entrance. She uttered an unladylike oath and stamped on the brake. In the dusky half-light she peered, slightly shaken, at a huge radiator which seemed about to swallow the little sports car in its giant maw.

A man came round the back of the car, glaring at her furiously. 'Do you always tear into blind openings like that?' he barked.

Selena got out of the car and endeavoured to retain her poise. 'I do when I'm the only person with any right to be here,' she said shortly. 'If you've come to see the house you should have made an appointment and, anyway, you're too late. It's already sold.'

The man continued to scowl at her. 'I know it is,' he said. 'I bought it.'

2

Taken aback, Selena stammered, 'Oh — I'm very sorry. I wasn't expecting you. I'm Selena Brent.'

The man took her offered hand. His scowl had faded, but he was still far from gushing. 'I'm Mark Denning. I drove up on impulse after Mr. Farmer told me this morning that my offer had been accepted. I'd never seen the house and I couldn't wait to get a look at it, so I picked up the keys and dashed over here.'

'I should have felt exactly the same. Although I don't think I would have bought a house without seeing it first. I'll just put my car out of the way, then I'll let you in.'

Selena backed her car out of the field and parked it along the lane in the lay-by. Returning to Mark Denning, she asked, 'Do you want to see the outside first?'

'I think I've done the outside fairly exhaustively, and it's damned cold. Let's go in.'

'I'm sorry I was out,' said Selena. 'But if you had keys, why didn't you let yourself in?'

'This is still your home, Mrs. Brent. As you weren't expecting me it would have been ill-mannered, if not down-right alarming for you to have found me here.'

Inside, Selena switched on the hall lights. In the dusk outside she hadn't been able to see Mark Denning at all clearly. His manner had not been quite what she had been expecting and, now that he was illuminated, neither was his appearance.

He was in his early thirties, around six feet tall, and his face was intelligent with wary grey eyes and a long sensitive mouth. In the damp air, his gold-brown hair flopped on to his forehead. He looked extremely cold.

'You look frozen. Would you like a cup of tea, or something?' she offered.

'Tea would be great.'

'It'll be warmer in the kitchen.' She led the way and switched on the lights, proud of the bright, welcoming room that sprang into view. 'Take off your coat. I'll whizz around and draw all the curtains while the kettle boils. That will warm the place up.'

* * *

She left him taking off his heavy overcoat and went to draw the curtains. In her own room she paused for a moment to look in the mirror. The black jumpsuit probably was over the top for Fairbridge, as Chrissie had implied but, seeing how it complemented her figure, she was glad that she had worn it. She hurried back to the kitchen to find Denning prowling around, examining the fittings in a proprietary fashion.

Selena made the tea and produced a plate of scones that Mrs. Hardy had made. 'Do you want to stay here?' she asked hesitantly. 'Or shall we go into the dining room?'

'This is fine.' He waited until she was seated at the kitchen table, then sat down at a distance from her. She was aware that he was studying her and, as she passed him his cup, he said, 'You come as something of a surprise, Mrs. Brent.'

'Oh, really? I understood Mr. Farmer had told you about me.'

'A lady's companion, he told me.' For the first time, Mark Denning's rather austere face relaxed into a smile. 'It sounded a bit lavender-and-lace. You don't quite fit the picture.'

Something in his expression caused Selena to blush slightly. 'Well, it's not exactly a profession. It's just something I took on temporarily.'

'And did you enjoy it?'

'Yes, I did.' Selena spoke defensively. 'I've been very happy here.' She buttered a couple of scones and pushed the plate towards him. 'Mr. Farmer said you wouldn't be living here all the time.'

'That's right. It would be too far from my business. I have a flat in London.' He bit into a scone. 'Mm. This is delicious!'

'Mrs. Hardy made them. She comes in daily to clean. She used to cook lunch every day when Miss Hallows was alive. She's a very good cook.' Selena broke off, sensing it was a little premature to advance Mrs. Hardy's case. At least the scones had made a good impression!

'Are there any other staff?'

'There's a part-time gardener, Mr. Jordan. I've laid him off for the time being. There isn't much to do at this time of year. He's a very good worker, although he's rather old.'

Mark Denning swallowed the last crumb of scone. 'Gardeners should be old,' he said sagely. 'Now, how about showing me over the house?'

'Of course.' Selena got to her feet and led the way back to the hall. 'You'll be familiar with the information in the printed brochure. The house as it stands is a major renovation, carried out in the 1580's, of a much older house. That's when it came into the Hallows family. A Thomas Hallows bought it — he was a cloth merchant and apparently quite prosperous.'

'Do you mean to say they could trace their family back that far?'

'Yes, they could, with one or two brief blank periods.'

'Are you connected with the family, Mrs. Brent?'

'Oh, no. Miss Hallows was the last of her line with the exception of her heir, a sort of second cousin, and he doesn't bear the name.'

'That's rather sad.'

'Yes, it is. Originally the house would have had a big central hall, two floors high, with a cross wing at each end. One wing would have contained the domestic quarters, kitchen, pantry and buttery, and the other wing the sleeping quarters.

'When Thomas bought the house we can guess, from the price he paid, that it was in a pretty dilapidated state. He divided the hall horizontally, which was being done generally at the time. The advent of chimneys meant that the fireplace need no longer have access to the sky.'

★ ★ ★

Selena indicated the cavernous inglenook with its glowing heap of logs. 'He built this fireplace in the back wall and did away with the earlier one in the centre of the hall. He also built chimneys in each end wall and had bigger windows put in the upper rooms. Apart from the present kitchen, the bathroom, central heating, and essential renovation, nothing basic has been altered since that time.'

Mark Denning seemed reluctant to leave the huge fireplace, but Selena led him on to the sitting room. 'This would have been the sleeping quarters, one big room. It was divided into two rooms around 1600.'

As they went on into the study, Denning asked, 'What about the furniture?'

'It's a mixture. Some of it is family furniture and the rest Miss Hallows bought from salerooms, mainly between the wars. Very little is contemporary with the house, obviously, but there are two seventeenth-century chests, one in the hall and one in a bedroom, and a dresser of that period in the dining room. Mr. Farmer said you might want to keep some of it.'

'Yes, that's right. It seems to fit in with the house very well. I'll have a proper look at it and decide what I want to make an offer for.'

Selena said hesitantly, 'There are a couple of things I should like to have, unless, of course, you wanted them.'

Denning smiled. 'Oh, I think I can allow you your first choice. Which were the things you wanted?'

'Well, this desk in here, and there's a little cabinet in my bedroom.'

Mark Denning looked at the desk

and the books that were piled on it. 'A lot of the books relate to the family, I see.'

'Yes, but most of those don't belong to the house. I borrowed them from the library, and the records office. I must take them back.'

★   ★   ★

He opened one of the books, examining the index. 'Were they for Miss Hallows' use or yours?'

'As a matter of fact, I was compiling a sort of history of the family. Chiefly to entertain Miss Hallows.'

'That's very interesting.'

'I found it so. I had just about finished getting all the threads together, but I hadn't got it into a final draft. There was a lot of research involved. I don't suppose it will be finished now.'

'It would be a shame if it wasn't. I don't know what your plans are, Mrs. Brent,' he went on, 'but I'd be very grateful if you could stay on for a time.

There will be things to co-ordinate and I shan't be able to spend a lot of time here. We could come to some financial arrangement, of course.'

'I haven't got anything definitely planned yet, but I had just succeeded in whipping up some enthusiasm in myself for a fresh start!'

'Of course. I understand.'

'What about — ' Selena hesitated. 'I mean, couldn't your wife stay at Cloudhallows?'

His face went suddenly impassive. 'I'm not married.'

'Well, I suppose I could stay for a while, until I decided what to do. In fact, it would suit me very well, and I certainly don't want any reimbursement.'

'I'd be very grateful. Of course — you being such an unusual lady's companion — I wouldn't expect to stay here at the same time.'

At a loss for a rejoinder, Selena said, 'What about Mrs. Hardy? Would you want me to keep her on?'

'Who? Oh, yes. Keep her on at the same terms, if that's agreeable to her.'

Reassured on that point, Selena led the way upstairs where she showed him the bedrooms and the fine timber beams.

Mark Denning displayed interest and pleasure in everything Selena pointed out, only wrinkling his nose slightly at the tiny bathroom.

At last they descended the stairs again. Back in the kitchen, Selena asked shyly, 'What do you think of your acquisition?'

'I like it very much. I liked it in the brochure and now it's come alive, no little thanks to you. You're an excellent guide. There are a few things to be done, of course,' he added.

'The bathroom?'

'Certainly the bathroom.' He smiled. 'Well, I'll soon get things moving. I'll be back again on Saturday, if that's OK with you.'

'Any time. I'll make sure I'm here.'

'I don't expect you to wait in for me,

if you don't object to me letting myself in?'

'Of course not.'

He shrugged into his coat and they stood facing each other for an awkward moment, each prepared to extend a hand, both wary of physical contact. Then he said goodbye and left the house swiftly.

As she watched his car turn into the lane, Selena's heart quickened. She was relieved, she told herself, that Cloud-hallows would be in good hands. Mark Denning had obviously liked the house and would not make too many drastic alterations. But, if she was honest, it wasn't only that. He had attracted her deeply. Not in the blatant, overwhelming way that Michael had; Mark Denning's deep, steady voice, the warmth in his eyes that accompanied his almost reluctant smile, had a subtly compelling effect.

She did her best to quench the flutter of excitement, collected her car from the lane and stowed it away beside the house. Then she made up the fire in the small sitting room and ate her supper in front of it, feeling alive in a way that she hadn't done for a long time.

★ ★ ★

The next morning she was singing about her chores when Mrs. Hardy arrived.

'You sound cheerful, love,' she said as she let herself in.

'I do feel a bit relieved. The new owner called yesterday and he seems very reasonable. He'd like you to stay on. And I can stay, too, for a while,' she finished, beaming.

'Oh, I am glad to hear that. And he seemed a nice gentleman, you say? What family has he got?'

'He hasn't any. At least he hasn't got a wife. He's not going to live here himself much of the time — just weekends, perhaps.'

Mrs. Hardy looked at her doubtfully. 'I know things are done differently nowadays, dear, but do you think you should stay here alone with him?'

'Things aren't done all that differently as far as I'm concerned. No, of course I can't. He made that point himself. I shall just stay until the house is ready for him to move in.'

'What's the matter with it as it is?'

'He liked it very much as it is, but I think he'll want a few things done. It is his house, after all. Maybe a second bathroom. He enjoyed your scones very much,' she added to Mrs. Hardy's faintly disapproving back.

Selena did some washing and tidied her room, then, to get out of Mrs. Hardy's way, decided to deliver the latest news to the Tremars. She slipped an anorak over her sweater and skirt and topped it with a knitted cap and muffler. She jogged along the lane to the village, and her cheeks were glowing and her eyes sparkling in the frosty air when she turned in at the Tremars' gate.

Chris was in the yard feeding the

dogs. She looked relieved at Selena's more homely outfit, and managed a cheerful greeting.

'Hello, Chrissie,' Selena said. 'I bring tidings of the new owner of Cloud-hallows. He turned up yesterday. Can you knock off for a minute?'

Chris reluctantly acknowledged that she could, shut up the pens and led the way into the house. In the kitchen she washed her hands and set out coffee cups.

Almost immediately, Stephen appeared from the front of the house. 'Hello, Selena. I thought I heard your voice.'

Chris' mouth tightened. 'Aren't you doing those innoculation records, Stephen?'

'Nearly finished. Is that coffee? I'm just ready for a cup.'

'I was telling Chris that the new owner turned up yesterday,' Selena said.

'Good heavens, that was quick. Were you expecting him?'

'No, but he was waiting in the garden when I got home from Tivenham yesterday tea-time. I nearly rammed his car.'

'Who is he?'

'His name is Mark Denning. I think he's from London. He seems very pleasant. In fact, I was quite favourably impressed.'

'In what way?'

'I suppose I was half expecting some brash, go-getting boor, but he was very interested in the house and its history.'

Chris plonked mugs of coffee unceremoniously in front of them. 'How old?'

'How old? How on earth do I know?'

'Well — forty? Sixty?'

'Oh, no. Early thirties, I would say.'

Stephen looked wary. 'What about family?'

'He doesn't seem to have any.'

'You'll be leaving then?' Chris queried with ill-concealed pleasure.

'No, as a matter of fact, he asked me to stay for the time being.'

'You can't do that!' Stephen was horrified. 'You can't stay at the house alone with him.'

Selena resisted an urge to point out that it would have been no different from their own situation. 'It'll only be until he moves in himself. He doesn't intend to live there all the time, anyway,' she said.

*　*　*

There was a long pause. At last Stephen said doubtfully, 'Well, of course, I'm very glad you're not going to be leaving yet.'

Looking anything but pleased, Chris said, 'Did you tell him about the road protest?'

'No, it didn't come up. He didn't stay very long. He's coming back on Saturday — I'll mention it then.'

'Ask him if he'd like to come over for drinks — or supper,' Stephen said. 'After all, we're going to be neighbours.'

'I'll ask him,' Selena promised, hoping that the Tremars wouldn't bore Mark Denning out of his mind with their road obsession.

58

She finished her coffee and, after talking for a few minutes longer, made her way back to Cloudhallows, going immediately to the study, and getting out the notes she had been working on. She had scarcely touched them since Miss Hallows died, but now she looked at them with renewed pleasure. Mark Denning's interest in the project had given her an incentive to finish it.

All the same, the days passed slowly, and it wasn't until Saturday that things began to liven up unexpectedly. Selena had just gone up to her room to change after working in the garden all morning when she heard the roar of a car engine in the lane. Cursing the fact that there hadn't been time to get out of her oldest sweater and jeans, she peeped out of a front bedroom window to see a racey, low-slung saloon outside the house. As she looked, a young woman got out and approached the front door.

Selena hurried downstairs and opened the door. The girl was tall, slim and strikingly attractive. She looked Selena up and down. 'Is this Cloudhallow House?'

'Cloudhallows. Yes, it is. But I'm afraid it's been withdrawn from auction,' Selena began.

'I know. I'm Fiona Sheridan, Mark Denning's personal assistant. Are you the caretaker?'

'I'm looking after the house.'

'Mrs. Brent, right? I expected a sort of Mrs. Danvers type.'

'Mrs. Danvers?'

'You know, darling — *Rebecca*.'

'Oh — yes. Well, come in, Miss Sheridan. Is there anything I can do?'

'Mark asked me to drive up and have a look at the house — to see what could be done with it. He seems to think I have a flair for that sort of thing. I completely re-designed his London office.'

★   ★   ★

She sauntered into the hall, dropping her driving gloves on to the chest. She wore cream ski-pants and a big black wool jacket.

60

'Would you like me to show you over the house, or would you prefer just to wander round?' Selena asked politely.

'You can give me the guided tour first but, my goodness, what a back-of-beyond hole! It took me nearly an hour to drive from London, and the last five miles are a maze.'

'There's a new road planned to begin next year. That will make the last part of the journey quicker.'

'Maybe Mark had that in mind. But, all the same, it's much too far from London.'

'Unless one wants to get away from London.'

Fiona looked at Selena uncomprehendingly. 'I suppose you've lived here all your life?'

'No, just for the last two years,' Selena said briefly. She started to show Fiona over the house, but with none of the pride she had felt with Mark Denning. And nothing about it seemed to appeal to Fiona. In the study she picked up a book Selena had been working with, read its title, and let it drop, scattering Selena's references.

'What business is Mr. Denning in?' Selena ventured as they ascended the stairs.

'He's a design engineer. It was my father's business then, two years ago, he bought Daddy out. Oh, good grief!'

Selena had been dreading Fiona's first sight of the bathroom but, all the same, she did feel that her shriek was rather overdone. 'I believe Mr. Denning intends to modernise it,' she murmured.

'Obliterate it, I hope you mean. Is it the only one?' Fiona demanded.

'I'm afraid so. Miss Hallows lived alone all her life until I came to stay with her. She didn't need more than one bathroom.'

* * *

Fiona's scarlet mouth turned down at the corners. 'I simply can't understand what possessed Mark, buying the place.

I only wish I'd known what he intended beforehand.'

'Didn't you?'

The suggestion that she was not completely in Denning's confidence seemed to irritate Fiona. 'Obviously, I knew he planned to buy a country house, but I thought it would be somewhere accessible — like Surrey.'

'Surrey would have been a lot more expensive.'

'He paid enough for this place.'

Selena was having increasing difficulty keeping her temper. 'He didn't need to pay so much,' she retorted. 'If he'd been prepared to wait for the auction, like everybody else, he would have got it for much less.'

'He'd probably have got it for next-to-nothing. I don't see anyone else being crazy enough to want it,' Fiona said rudely.

Aware that her cheeks were flushed and her eyes flashing, Selena took a deep breath and said, 'On the contrary, several people were interested. I, myself, would have gone over the reserve price for it.'

Fiona shot her a surprised glance. 'What about all this old furniture? When will you be getting rid of it?'

'Mr. Denning wants to have a good look at it. Anything he doesn't want will go to auction.'

'Well, I certainly intend to put my foot down about that! I suppose the purchase of the house is a *fait accompli*, but the furniture will have to go. As it is, I'll need flair amounting to genius to make anything of it. I've seen enough Mrs. — er — I have to fly, I have an engagement in town.'

She clattered downstairs, leaving a drift of expensive, heavy perfume in her wake. Seething, Selena banged the door behind her. What part did she play in Mark Denning's life? she wondered. She had acted in a very proprietary fashion over the house but, if she was his fiancée, she would surely have announced herself as such. Perhaps she was hoping things would move in that direction. The fact that Mark Denning's business had, until recently, belonged to her father, could make her possessive towards that and, by extension, everything else concerning him. In addition to which she was obviously a spoiled brat.

Selena tried to regain her good spirits of the past few days, but had failed. Her feet drew her to the study, and then to the desk. Without thinking what she was doing, she stowed her work back into the drawer again and stacked up the books into a neat pile.

3

By bedtime, Selena had talked herself into a more reasonable frame of mind. Mark Denning's representatives, no matter how abrasive their personalities, were no business of hers. It had been foolish of her to imagine that because Denning had said he had no wife he was as uncommitted as she was.

The next morning she was reading the paper over a cup of coffee when, at eleven o'clock, she heard a car stop in the passing-place in the lane. Her heartbeat quickened a little and she checked her appearance in a glass-fronted cupboard as she went to open the door.

Mark Denning was coming up the short drive. Selena smiled at him. 'Good morning. I heard the car.'

'I'm sorry I couldn't make yesterday.'

'That's all right. I'm just having

66

coffee. Would you like a cup?'

'Yes, please.' He followed her into the kitchen and sat down where he had sat on his previous visit. 'I believe Miss Sheridan has been to look at the house?' he said.

'Yes.' There was a pause. 'I don't think she liked it,' Selena said flatly, passing him his coffee.

He looked at her ruefully. 'That was the impression I got. It's not exactly her scene. She tells me that, in your opinion, I bid over the odds for the house.'

'That was the general opinion.'

'It was exactly what I wanted. I don't mind paying to get that.'

'How gratifying to be able to.'

He glanced at her quickly. 'Fiona also told me that you were in the market for the house.'

'Yes, that's true.'

'You were in a position to buy it?'

'I was in a position to pay a reasonable price for it.'

The atmosphere between them had

suddenly become guarded. Mark said, 'I'm sorry. I had no idea. Any other prospective buyers I've antagonised?'

'You haven't antagonised me in the least, Mr. Denning. There are plenty of other houses, perhaps in less of what Miss Sheridan terms a 'back-of-beyond hole'. I've no idea who else would have bid at auction for Cloudhallows. The local vet, Stephen Tremar, was interested, I believe.'

'Well — ' Mark Denning produced a large notebook from his pocket — 'since I have bought it, I've made a few preliminary notes of things to get started on. First of all, is the house listed? Fiona tells me the grade of listing makes all the difference to what one is allowed to do.'

'Damn Fiona,' Selena thought. Aloud she said, 'Cloudhallows isn't listed, so you and Miss Sheridan are free to do anything you like to it.'

'I'm not a vandal, Mrs. Brent. I didn't buy the house in order to ruin it. Now, Fiona also tells me that there's to be a new road. Where exactly would that run?'

'The other side of the plantation, where the Westingham lane runs now.'

★   ★   ★

He pushed aside his coffee cup and sketched rapidly on his pad. A professional-looking plan of Cloudhallows, its ground, and the lane appeared. 'Could you draw it in for me?'

He handed Selena the pen. To reach the pad she had to lean against him and she was painfully aware of his arm pressed against her body, and his cheek close to hers.

She said a little breathlessly, 'Drawing's not my best talent, I'm afraid.' She drew in a rather shaky line. 'Somewhere about there.'

He studied her effort. 'Will it interfere with the property at all?'

'There will probably be colossal disturbance while it's being built,' she replied. 'After that, the trees will screen it from sight and, I should imagine, cut out most of the sound. However, there is a strong protest against it in the village. Stephen had hoped that you would add your weight to it.'

'Stephen?'

'Stephen Tremar, the vet.'

'What's his interest?'

'He owns the house on the corner — ' Selena indicated its position on the map — 'although it's rented at present.'

'The road wouldn't seem to affect that house much.'

'No, not so much as Cloudhallows and, of course, it's not a house of such quality. That's why he thought your support would be valuable.'

'The road has to go somewhere.'

'That's what the Ministry keeps telling us. We say, why here?'

'Is there an alternative?'

'Yes. On the other side of the river, south of the village.' Once more she leant against him and felt her head swim. 'Along here,' she said, drawing on his sketch.

He shuffled his notes together with uncharacteristically clumsy fingers and stuffed them into his jacket pocket. Suddenly Selena was sure that he was as intensely aware of her nearness as she was of his.

He cleared his throat and said brusquely, 'Well, obviously, I don't know the lay-out. I don't see that the road will inconvenience me greatly behind the trees, and I would have thought the second alternative would be a greater eyesore to the village. I'll have to look into it. Meanwhile, the first two priorities about the house are garaging and bathroom facilities. I shall need a three-car garage.' He glanced at her. 'I'll have a look around and try to get the most unobtrusive siting. I knew nothing of the new road but, if it passes near, I'll have a new drive laid to emerge into it, if permitted. That will dispense with some of the traffic in this narrow lane. Inside the house, I'll start by extending the existing bathroom into the upper hall and installing a new suite. And I propose to turn the smallest bedroom into a second bath-room.

'I realise, Mrs. Brent,' he continued, 'it won't be pleasant living among the upheaval. If you still feel you want to stay on, I insist on you accepting a salary. And the cleaner must be given extra hours and an improved rate of pay to cope with the work.' He paused. 'What do you say?'

'I'll try it for the time being.'

'I'm very grateful. The surveyor and a plumber will arrive at ten tomorrow morning, if that's all right with you?'

'I'll be here to let them in.' Selena smiled wickedly. 'Shouldn't Miss Sheridan be here to — er — exercise her flair?'

He grinned back at her. 'Fiona does her thing at a later stage. She distances herself while walls are being bashed down! Now, if you'll excuse me, I'll make another quick tour.'

★ ★ ★

He left the kitchen and Selena heard him bounding up the stairs. She washed up their coffee cups thoughtfully. He seemed to have changed since their first encounter. Pride of possession or, perhaps, Fiona's influence, seemed to have made him more ruthless towards Cloudhallows. His driving-all-before-him enthusiasm reminded her of Michael. His plans might be no more than to make the house more comfortable and convenient, but she certainly wouldn't stand by and see it desecrated.

She was still pottering about in the kitchen when he reappeared twenty minutes later.

'I won't bother you any longer. Are you sure it's no trouble to let the workmen in tomorrow?'

'Quite sure. Either Mrs. Hardy or I will be here. By the way, Stephen Tremar asked me to pass on an invitation for drinks any time you're in the neighbourhood.'

'Oh, thanks. Tell him I'd be glad to come.'

'I ought to warn you, he'll probably try to pressurise you into joining his anti-road protest. He's pretty enthusiastic.'

Mark Denning's mobile mouth took on a stubborn line. 'I'm sure he'll understand if I get my bearings before I commit myself.'

'Of course,' Selena said, though inwardly doubtful.

He smiled his damnably attractive smile and left. Selena cooked herself a meal then ate it reflectively with a glass of wine. After she had washed her dishes, she set out to walk to the Tremars.

She found them slumped in front of the TV, watching an old movie. Stephen welcomed her in, switching off the set.

'Have you seen any more of the mystery man?' Chris asked.

Selena sat down by the fire, stretching her fingers to the blaze. 'Yes, he was at the house this morning.'

'You sound a bit doubtful. Isn't he such a paragon after all?' asked Chris.

'Well, he certainly seemed more of a dynamo today. He unveiled his plans for Cloudhallows: second bathroom, and enlarging the existing one — that's quite reasonable — and a three-car garage and a new drive.'

'Where is he planning the new drive?' Stephen asked.

'Probably down to meet the new road.'

'So he doesn't object to it?'

'He wants to reserve judgment until he understands the situation. My feeling is he won't object.'

'Damn!' Stephen lapsed into a sulky silence.

'Maybe you can talk him round, Stephen,' Chris put in. 'You're so persuasive when you put all the facts in front of people.' She turned to Selena. 'Did you pass on our invitation?'

'Yes, I did.'

'A three-car garage!' Stephen exploded. 'It will be as big as the house.'

'I suppose it could go into that little dell behind the house,' Selena said.

'The trees would mask it.'

'A man like that! He'll probably put it in the front garden!'

Selena managed to refrain from retorting that they had no idea what sort of a man he was. Instead she said, 'His personal assistant came to see the house yesterday. Maybe she put ideas into his head. She's a very forceful young woman. A sort of Sloane Ranger type.'

'I don't know why on earth you're staying on there,' Stephen said.

'It's just that it's convenient. I'd like to get a job before I think of buying a house. I don't want to live on capital. Obviously, if it looks as though Mr. Denning means to ruin Cloudhallows, I'll leave.'

★   ★   ★

They talked a little while longer, then Stephen walked back to Cloudhallows with Selena. At the door she asked him in, half hoping that he would refuse, but he followed her into the hall and pulled her into his arms. Before she could stop him he was kissing her passionately.

When she had gently freed herself, he said, 'I'm sorry, Selena, but you must know how I feel about you.'

'Yes, Stephen, I do. I'm sorry, too, but I don't want this yet.'

'What is it, darling? Don't you feel ready to take another chance after Michael?'

'I suppose that's it.' It was a face-saving response, and one that, until the last few days, she would have thought true.

'I couldn't bear not to see you, but I won't put any pressure on you,' said Stephen, releasing her reluctantly. 'More than anything in the world I would like to live here at Cloudhallows with you. What a pity the old lady didn't leave it to you.'

Selena stared at him, stunned. 'Stephen, that's just ridiculous! We were very close, but I only knew her for two years. What's two years out of a life of eighty? Besides, she knew I had money of my own.'

'Unfortunately not quite enough,' Stephen mumbled, but he could see his remark had offended Selena and quite soon he left. She watched him trudge disconsolately down the lane and wished he could fall for Chris, who doted on him and would have made him such a good wife. Why did life have to be so unfair?

* * *

During the evening she took down the bathroom curtains and cleared it of oddments, ready for the arrival of the workmen. They were on the doorstep at nine the following morning. They surveyed, traced pipes, drank tea and departed at eleven.

'Call that a day's work!' Mrs. Hardy was heard to comment loudly.

But the next day a new team arrived. The furniture was moved from the smallest bedroom and the floorboards taken up. At five o'clock, just as the men were loading up their truck, Mark Denning arrived.

'Been helping them?' he asked cheekily, reaching out a hand towards her face and producing a lump of plaster from her hair.

She laughed breathlessly. His hand, warm and gentle, had touched her cheek. 'No, only the usual woman's role. Keeping the cups of tea flowing!'

'British workmen run on it. You mustn't deprive them.'

There was a pause while they stood smiling at each other, pleased with what they saw. Then Mark said, 'Would you like to come out for a meal with me?'

Selena flushed. 'Really, you don't have to — '

'I know I don't, but I have to eat somewhere.' His tone was almost brusque. 'You must be ready to get out of the house.'

'I admit the hammering is still ringing in my ears! Can you wait while I have a quick bath? Oh!' Her eyes widened in dismay. 'I haven't got a bath.'

'I'm sorry. It shouldn't be for long.'

'Well, it will just have to be the kitchen sink. Er — would you mind waiting for me elsewhere?'

★ ★ ★

Selena collected her toilet things, her robe and a towel, and looked rapidly through her wardrobe. Finally she decided on black velvet slacks and a peach silk blouse. She washed in the kitchen, changed and made up her face, before joining him in the sitting room. She saw admiration flare in his eyes to be quickly masked. This was not a man who liked to show his feelings.

To ease the moment she said, 'It occurs to me that we're very early for dinner, Mr. Denning. Should we call at the Tremars for that drink first?'

He didn't look very keen, but he said, 'That seems a good idea. And for heaven's sake, won't you call me Mark?'

She smiled agreement and they went out to his car. She directed him the short distance to the Tremars' house, where they found the cousins just finishing tea. When the introductions had been made, Chris produced coffee and brandy with some animation.

'We've been looking forward so much to meeting you,' she gushed. 'Miss Hallows was a sweet old thing, but she didn't contribute much to village life.'

Stephen's feelings at seeing Selena with Mark were obvious on his guileless face. 'You don't intend living at Cloudhallows full-time, I understand, Mr. Denning?'

'I don't think that will be practical. I need to be nearer to my work — and social contacts. Perhaps when the new road is built — '

Selena groaned inwardly. It was the signal for Stephen to begin and, for the next half-hour, Mark was lectured on the violation of Cloudhallows, village life and the general environment. Selena tried to steer the conversation to more general ground, but finally gave up and said, 'Maybe we should be leaving, Mark, if you're going back to town tonight.'

The familiar 'Mark' stopped Stephen in full spate. He said stiffly, 'I'm very sorry, Mr. Denning. We're boring you to death when you've scarcely arrived.'

Mark didn't refute it. 'Well, I can see feeling is running high. I don't think the road will bother me much personally — '

'You won't be living there, will you?' Chris interrupted with her usual gauche bluntness.

'As for the wider issues of disturbance to the village and the countryside,' Mark continued as though she hadn't spoken, 'obviously I shall want to study the position for myself before I come to any decision.'

Chris had flushed an unattractive red, but Stephen appeared to accept Mark's response. 'Of course. But we hope you'll come to see our point of view and lend your support.'

They shook hands in reasonable

amity, and Selena and Mark returned to the car. Once seated, he looked at her in wry amusement.

'I'm sorry,' she said. 'I did warn you, but I didn't think they would come on as strong as that.'

'I suppose, living in a small village, one does get passionately involved in issues that don't seem as pressing to outsiders. Now, where would you like to eat?'

'We don't actually have much choice. There's the Bull at Rimington. 'Good pub fare'.'

'That sounds OK. Will you direct me?'

★   ★   ★

Selena settled down in the comfortable seat and guided him round the four miles of winding lanes. The Bull was a big old coaching inn, attractively modernised. Although she had been there a few times with Stephen, Selena had forgotten, or never noticed, the close intimacy of the dining-tables. The waitress led them to a candle-lit alcove for two.

'Is this all right?' Selena asked Mark doubtfully.

'Sure, fine.' He helped her out of her jacket and she sat down opposite him at the tiny table. His face was thrown into interesting planes and shadows by the candlelight. He was no more conventionally good-looking than Stephen, certainly less flamboyantly handsome than Michael, but the shrewd, intelligent grey eyes, suggesting both humour and an austere coolness, fascinated her.

'Did you say that Mr. Tremar had been interested in buying Cloud-hallows?' Mark asked, when they'd chosen their food.

'Yes, they want more room than they have now. Chris particularly wants to expand her dog breeding, and start an animal sanctuary — '

'Oh, no, don't tell me I've gazumped an animal sanctuary. Little disadvantaged doggies gazing at me reproachfully!'

84

Selena giggled. 'No, you haven't done that. Stephen couldn't raise the capital unless he sold his old family home. That's the big, shabby house on the corner of the lane.'

'Couldn't he use that for his animals? It would seem much more suitable than Cloudhallows.'

'Yes, it is, but Chris rented it while Stephen was at college, presumably before she decided on her dog breeding, and now they have sitting tenants that they can't get rid of — the Reardons. The children are rather wild. You mustn't let them make a nuisance of themselves.'

The waitress brought their starters and Mark applied himself to his soup. After a moment he said, 'You didn't consider — a merger with Stephen Tremar? As you both wanted the house, I mean?'

Selena looked directly at him. 'John Farmer asked me that. The answer is no.'

He looked a little abashed as he

poured the wine. 'Sorry, but I can't help being curious. And Stephen Tremar is obviously dotty about you.'

Selena was annoyed to find herself blushing. She concentrated on her melon, then, to turn the tables on him, observed, 'Miss Sheridan seems a very efficient girl.'

'Oh, she is. She's made herself invaluable. She has a really good business brain.'

His enthusiasm induced a quite unreasonable depression in Selena, who said, 'She told me that your business had belonged to her father.'

Mark seemed less enchanted over that. 'Yes, it did. Confidentially, it's a little difficult sometimes for them to realise that it's changed hands! But I don't think he would have sold out if Fiona hadn't been in my corner. He'd turned down several bigger concerns.'

They had started on their second courses when Mark said, 'Would you mind if I asked you about your husband?'

'That would rather depend on what you asked.'

'Are you divorced? Widowed?'

'Divorced — two years ago. I married early.'

'And what happened? Were you too young to settle down?'

Selena laughed shortly. 'No, it was nothing like that. Settling down wasn't even an option.'

He was watching her, waiting for elucidation, but she said, 'I'm sorry. I don't feel like talking about it.'

'I'm sorry I brought it up.' He filled their glasses. 'The man was obviously an idiot.'

*　*　*

Mark's remark, uttered with no hint of flirtation, threw Selena completely. She took a quick drink of her wine, choking slightly over it. Again to put the ball in his court, she said, 'And you? Have you ever been married?'

The change in his face was almost

alarming. In a second, his easy confident expression became bitter. 'Oh yes,' he said. 'I was married, but my wife got out when the going was rough.'

There was a painful silence, then Mark laughed shame facedly. 'It seems that neither of us is quite ready to talk on that particular subject, so let's change it. Tell me more about Cloud-hallows.'

Relieved that the conversation had turned less personal, Selena started on her subject with enthusiasm and Mark listened with interest. Only when they were drinking their coffee did she falter apologetically. 'I'm sorry. I'm afraid I've been boring you. I get carried away.'

'On the contrary, you make it all come alive. To someone with my kind of lifestyle, it gives a sense of continuity to be aware of these age-old dwellings and the long succession of people who lived in them. Sometimes it seems I scarcely have time to think. I hope that at Cloudhallows I'll have a chance to come to terms with myself.'

He smiled at her and she felt her knees turn to water. In the intimacy of the little booth it was as though they held their breath, both aware that they were on the brink of something devastating.

'Some more wine?' Mark asked.

Selena shook her head. 'No, thanks. Perhaps we should be going. You have a long drive back to town.'

They left the restaurant and drove slowly back to Cloudhallows through the frosty night, under a brilliantly starlit sky. Mark stopped the car at the gate and once again they were paralysed by the force of their mutual attraction.

Selena cleared her throat. 'Do you want to come in for a minute?'

'No.' His voice was husky. 'As you say, I have a long drive home.'

He opened the door for Selena and she walked up to the front door. As she opened it, the car disappeared down the lane.

She closed the door and leant against it, hugging her arms around her body although the house was warm. 'I wanted him to come in,' she thought. 'I wanted him to stay.' The admission shocked her. It wasn't her way. But it had seemed natural that they should be together; it was his house, they had eaten and drunk well, they were tired.

She slipped off her shoes and curled up in a chair in front of the dying fire. 'I must be careful,' she reminded herself. 'He could be a ruthless man, one used to getting his own way.' There was something of Michael in him and she was determined not to be hurt like that ever again.

★ ★ ★

The following morning brought the workmen again. First the plumbers who had to be supplied with copious draughts of tea then, as soon as they had been firmly shooed upstairs, a new team who began clearing and levelling the ground for the garage foundations.

Somewhere in the middle of the

upheaval Mrs. Hardy arrived.

'Isn't half some goings-on,' she announced. 'Miss Hallows would turn in her grave.'

'Good morning, Mrs. Hardy.' Selena smiled.

'Good morning, love.' Mrs. Hardy tied on her floral apron. 'What's the point of me doing any cleaning, I should like to know? Dust everywhere. I did all the windows last week and look at them now.'

'I know, it does seem pointless,' Selena sympathised. 'Why don't you just give the kitchen a good do and call it a day? You'll have plenty of work when the men leave.'

'When will that be, I wonder?' Mrs. Hardy rolled her eyes heavenwards. 'I don't know how you can stand it here all the time, but you look as if you're thriving on it.'

Selena avoided the older woman's eyes. 'I don't expect it will be for much longer. Mr. Denning called yesterday and seemed pleased with the way the work was going.'

'Oh, he was here, was he?'

'Yes, about tea-time. I took him to meet the Tremars and then we went out for a meal.'

'That was nice, dear. Wouldn't it be lovely if we could fix him up with Miss Chrissie? Stop her mooning over poor Mr. Stephen all the time!' said Mrs. Hardy.

'And fix me up with Stephen,' Selena thought to herself. 'Neatly pigeon-holed in Mrs. Hardy's romantic imagination.'

★ ★ ★

The work inside the house proceeded at a good pace and, by the end of the week, both bathrooms were completed and elegantly furnished, and numerous small repair jobs had been carried out. Outside the house, the ground had been cleared and the foundation for the garage laid. Mark had not come back again, although Selena found herself constantly listening for him. But when, the following Saturday afternoon, the sound of a car engine brought her hurrying to the window, once again it was Fiona who alighted from her car.

Looking very glamorous in a suit of soft light blue suede, she sauntered up the path, pushed open the door and called out, 'Hi, there!'

Selena came into the hall. 'Hello, Miss Sheridan.'

'Oh, *Fiona*, please! I've come to inspect progress. How is our country retreat coming along?'

The 'our' gave Selena a sudden little blow to the heart. 'The bathrooms are finished,' she said, quickly regaining her composure.

'Well, that's a start. I'll go up **and** have a look at them.' She ran lightly up the stairs, checking first the restyled old bathroom, then bursting into Selena's bedroom without apology before she found the new one.

When she came downstairs again she said, almost reluctantly, 'They seem to have made a good job of it. And fast, too. How surprising to find decent workmanship out here.'

'Actually, it's where I would expect to find it.'

'What an improvement.' Fiona smiled at Selena patronisingly. 'You won't know yourself after living in such primitive conditions. But I think we ought to consider finding a room for a sauna, or at least a Jacuzzi. Maybe the back bedroom next to the old bathroom. I'll talk to Mark about it.'

'*My* bedroom,' Selena thought, then remembered that she was only at Cloudhallows on borrowed time. But she was unable to stop herself saying, 'I thought Mr. Denning might come to see how things are going.'

'He's abroad, darling. Hamburg. What about the garage and the new drive?'

'The foundation for the garage is laid. Surely Mr. Denning won't go ahead with the drive until he's certain of the route of the new road? It could lead to nowhere.'

'If Mark wants the new road to pass near his property, I think you'll find that it will.'

'Believe me, Miss Sheridan, it's not easy to influence a government ministry.'

'Well, in that case, we'll have to go for a helicopter pad.'

Selena's mouth fell open. 'A helicopter pad? You're joking!'

'Not at all. Fast communication is vital in the business world. It's quite ridiculous the time it takes to reach here. I shall certainly mention a helicopter pad to Mark.'

'But that's monstrous! The noise would be intolerable, not only for Cloudhallows, but for the whole neighbourhood.'

'Too bad,' said Fiona laconically. 'Fairbridge will have to be dragged kicking into the twentieth century. Anyhow, it won't concern you, will it? You'll be on your way now that you're no longer needed to supervise the workmen in the house.'

'Yes, I'll be leaving soon,' Selena said quietly.

'Jolly good.' Fiona beamed at her. 'Actually, I plan to spend some time here myself in the better weather. A rustic idyll. Might be rather fun.'

★ ★ ★

She went back to her car, slid into the driving seat, pulled her long legs in after her, and waved a hand as she roared off.

Selena gazed after her. 'I think you just got your marching orders, my girl,' she told herself. It looked as if Fiona had learned of her evening with Mark and had decided to nip any further fraternising in the bud. Any hostessing at Cloudhallows was clearly going to be done by her.

A moment later Stephen drew up at the gate. He got out of his car and kissed Selena. 'Who was the ravishing brunette who took the corner like a bat out of hell?'

'That is Miss Fiona Sheridan, Mark Denning's trouble-shooter. She thinks Cloudhallows needs a helicopter pad.'

'Good grief, you're not serious!'

'I think I am. The new road may not be fast enough.'

'For what?'

'It's called living in the fast lane. I've done plenty of it myself, in my time. A sauna and a Jacuzzi are other possibilities.'

He followed her into the house. 'What awful people! Why buy the place, then set out to change its whole character?'

'Well, they haven't done it yet, and the bathrooms *are* lovely. Mark doesn't seem so bad, but Miss Sheridan appears to have an unfortunate influence on him.'

'That's rubbish, Selena. She's only his employee.'

Selena was about to defend Mark further, but Stephen was watching her, so she merely said, 'Are you on your way somewhere?'

'No, I'm coming back from Seamer's Farm.'

'Stay and have some tea.'

They went into the kitchen together. 'We haven't seen anything of you all week,' said Stephen.

'I've had to stay around here. I've been at the beck and call of workmen.'

'I hope Denning is paying you for this.'

'I have my accommodation. That's more than a fair exchange for what I do.'

* * *

Stephen looked unmollified as Selena set the table. She quickly made some sandwiches and brought out a fruit cake. As she passed Stephen his tea he said, a little sulkily, 'How was your date last Sunday night?'

'It was hardly a date! It was very pleasant. As I said, Mark seems a perfectly reasonable man, sensitive to Cloudhallows — '

'It sounds like it — a helicopter pad!' Stephen snorted through a mouthful of sandwich. 'When is he moving in, anyway?'

'He hasn't said. Apparently Miss Sheridan intends to spend time here, too.'

'You won't like that. Selena, why don't you move out and leave Cloud-hallows to them? It will never be the same again. Come and stay with us until you find a place to live. We've got a spare bedroom.'

'Thank you, Stephen, but I'm all right here for the time being. Once Mark and — and Miss Sheridan move in, I'll leave. I imagine they'll expect me to. I'm going to start looking for a job.'

'Where?'

'Tivenham, I suppose, although there isn't much going there. Perhaps a bit further afield, Oxford, or Birmingham.'

Stephen stared moodily into his cup. 'I can't bear to think of this place without you. I suppose it's no good asking if you'd reconsider marrying me.'

'No, Stephen,' Selena said gently.

'Would it make a difference if I had more cash? You have money —'

'I'm not an heiress. I sold a modest family home, that's all. No, it wouldn't make any difference. I had years of financial trouble with Michael. It wasn't that that ended the marriage.'

'I'm sorry. I shouldn't have said that. But when I see that Denning chap flashing around in his big car, sweeping you off your feet —'

'Oh, Stephen, I'm just letting his workmen in!' But once again she avoided his eye for fear he should see how his words had struck home.

★   ★   ★

The following week was quiet at Cloudhallows. The outside builders continued work on the garage. Jordan, the gardener, truculent at the best of times, dug and hoed in a fury of resentment, his back pointedly turned to the intruders. Inside the house, Mrs.

Hardy and Selena cleaned and polished until the old house gleamed. Once again, on the Friday, Fiona descended in her upsetting whirl. Mr. Denning, she announced, intended to invite two business contacts to Cloudhallows shortly. Was everything ready?

'When?' Selena had asked nervously.

'Probably in two weeks.' Was there sufficient decent crockery, glassware and linen? Fiona had gone on to enquire. She could send down services from London. Two portable televisions would be arriving for the guest bedrooms.

Selena responded that she thought the house was adequately equipped, and Fiona had flashed off again, leaving her in a state of quandary and agitation.

What was to be her role? Was she expected to play hostess, or make herself scarce? What about catering? Was Mrs. Hardy to do the cooking? She had a phone number for Mark and, after much hesitation, she rang it. She was answered by a secretary who said he was at a meeting and would call her back.

Selena stayed near the phone for most of the day until, at five o'clock, Mark returned her call.

'It won't be for at least two weeks yet,' Mark replied to her questions. 'I'll give you plenty of notice. I wouldn't be sending people down without discussing it with you. I don't, of course, expect you to do anything. As for the catering, Mrs. Hardy can undertake it if she's capable. Otherwise Fiona will do it. She's a *Cordon Bleu* cook.'

'Wouldn't she just be,' thought Selena. She said hesitantly, 'Do you want me to move out while they're here?'

'Not unless you want to. Look, please don't worry about anything. There was no need for Fiona to mention it yet, but I expect she thought she should check to see that everything was ready.'

When he rang off, Selena was still not reassured. While she was still living at Cloudhallows, she couldn't help feeling responsible.

★ ★ ★

The next morning was a lot warmer, with a feel of spring in the air. There were crocuses to be seen among the clustered snowdrops, their heads bright against the black earth.

Mrs. Hardy said on her arrival, 'Didn't hardly need my coat today. Proper spring day it is.'

As she clattered her tools out of the cupboard, Selena said to her, 'We're to expect two guests shortly, Mrs. Hardy.'

'What, here?'

'Yes. Probably in a couple of weeks' time. Business contacts of Mr. Denning's.'

'Will I have to cook for them?'

'Not if you don't want to. Miss Sheridan can do it.'

Mrs. Hardy looked worried. 'Well, I don't know, Selena. I've only ever been a plain cook, as you know. Suppose these gentlemen are foreigners and want exotic dishes?'

'Oh, I think Mr. Denning would have

mentioned it if they were. He stressed that we were not to worry.'

'He won't be so casual if things don't go right,' Mrs. Hardy warned.

'Well, if you're at all concerned, we can ask Miss Sheridan. She seems to be extremely efficient. She wanted to know if we were adequately supplied for guests.'

Mrs. Hardy went off to check the store cupboards, torn between a sense of responsibility for the cooking and a reluctance to hand over the kitchen to a strange woman.

On Monday morning, Selena made a trip to Tivenham to obtain what was needed, in the best quality available in the small town, getting receipts for Mark Denning. On Friday afternoon Mark himself paid an unannounced visit. He was strolling round the garden when Selena went out to greet him.

'You've been gardening,' he said. 'It looks lovely.'

'Oh, only the fiddly bits. Mr. Jordan has been in for a couple of days doing the heavy stuff.' She hesitated. 'Would you like to see the guest bedrooms? I think we have everything we need. The bed linen and towels are old, but better quality than you can buy nowadays.'

He followed her in from the sunny garden and they went upstairs together. The bed linen in the two guest rooms was, as Selena had said, beautiful with handmade lace on the snowy linen sheets and pillowcases. Thick, fluffy towels waited on the mahogany towel rails. There were posies of spring flowers on the gleaming chests of drawers, and freshly laundered curtains at the windows.

'It all looks perfect,' Mark approved. 'A real country home. I can't thank you enough.'

'I haven't done anything special. Miss Hallows liked it to look like this. I'm still a little apprehensive about your guests, though, and Mrs. Hardy is scared out of her wits,' she confessed.

'There's absolutely no need to be. What I would like from her is food to match the house. Would that be possible?'

'Oh, yes, I think so,' Selena said with a little more confidence than she felt. 'How long do you expect your guests to stay?'

'Three nights at most, but more likely only two.'

'Are you sure I won't be in the way here? There's not a lot of room.'

'Are you joking? You're my chief asset!'

His tone was lightly bantering. Then their eyes met and, in a moment, the whole atmosphere changed. They stood very still, close together, scarcely breathing. Mark put out a hand and lightly touched her arm. 'Selena?' he said gently. Inexorably their bodies drew together. From outside a car door was slammed savagely and the spell was broken. Selena drew her breath shakily and they both looked out of the window.

★ ★ ★

They saw that Mark's car had somehow run out of the field and across the lane, where it rested, its nose buried in the far hedge, completely blocking the road. Stephen's car was stopped, almost touching it. He looked angrily towards the house then, seeing them together at the bedroom window, his expression grew thunderous.

'That's a stupid thing to do, isn't it, Denning?' he yelled.

Mark stifled an oath and ran downstairs and out into the lane, Selena following him.

'How did that happen?' he muttered, looking at the car.

'I imagine it happened because you forgot to put the handbrake on.' Stephen was still fuming.

'I wouldn't do that — '

'Well, it isn't on now,' Stephen announced with what Selena thought rather childish triumph.

Still looking bewildered, Mark slid across to the driver's seat. 'Well, I can't think how it happened, but I'm very sorry, Mr. Tremar.'

'It's a good thing I take these lanes at a reasonable speed. If I belted round them in the way some people do we'd have had a couple of write-offs,' said Stephen.

Selena watched Mark back his car into the field again, wishing that Stephen would stop his self-righteous monologue.

There was a pause of some seconds before Mark emerged from the car, gingerly holding between his fingers a half-consumed stick of toffee.

'And I don't suck toffee-bars while I'm forgetting to put the brake on,' he said.

Selena and Stephen looked at each other. 'Shane Reardon!' they exclaimed together.

'He's one of the Reardon brood who live on the corner,' Selena expanded. 'They're a thoroughly undisciplined mob, and Shane is mad about cars.'

'Might have been more sensible to lock it, old man,' Stephen said.

'It was on my land.'

There was a general impasse. Selena didn't know whether Stephen had been intending to call on her, or was only passing, or whether Mark was about to leave. Finally she said, 'Were you coming to see me, Stephen?'

'I was just on my way home from a call and thought I'd look in for a minute. However, if you're busy — '

'I was just leaving,' Mark said quickly. He turned to Selena. 'Thank you again for making the house so attractive. Particularly after all the mess. And please don't worry about my guests. I know I can rely on you to have the place warm and comfortable.'

4

As soon as Mark had driven off, Stephen said, 'You seem to be getting very thick with him.'

'I've hardly seen him. He just called in to keep an eye on progress.'

'And make some!'

'Don't be ridiculous, Stephen. He wanted to see how the garage was coming along.'

'In the bedroom?'

Selena flushed angrily. 'If you're just going to make cheap cracks, you'd better go.'

She turned for the door, but Stephen headed her off.

'I'm sorry, it's none of my business. But it's been a rotten day. I was wrestling for an hour with that foul-tempered mare of Brownings, and then another hour with Browning, who was trying to get something off my bill. Farmers seem to think they have a right never to settle bills.'

He looked so wretched that Selena took pity on him. She knew he was on a tight financial rein. 'Come in and have some coffee.'

He kicked off his muddy shoes gloomily and followed Selena into the kitchen. As she set out the cups, he said, 'You haven't forgotten the meeting tomorrow night?'

Selena sighed inwardly. She had been very much hoping to be allowed to forget it. Without doubt, it would be comprised of the same old long-winded arguments churned out by the same all-purpose protesters. She said, 'I really don't think there's much point in going on with it, Stephen. I'm afraid it's a lost cause.'

The sullen expression returned to Stephen's face. 'Denning has been getting at you, hasn't he? You used to be as committed as any of us.'

'He hasn't been getting at me. As for his own point of view, I don't think he sees — '

'He doesn't see what's in it for him, so he's not interested. I know his type.'

'Well, I don't — I don't know anything about him. But don't let's quarrel, Stephen. Of course I'll come to the meeting. I'll call for you at seven-thirty.'

He drank his coffee in moody silence and, as Selena watched his car roar away, she reflected that Mark had unwittingly driven a wedge between them. It wasn't his fault — he probably had no interest in her — but her position in his house was obviously upsetting to Stephen.

* * *

The meeting in the village hall the following evening was as boring and time-wasting as Selena had foreseen. In addition to Stephen and Chrissie Tremar there were only five others present. Miss Blunt, the good-natured village postmistress, dragooned there by Chrissie, Miss Markham, the village eccentric, eighty-year-old Colonel Brittan, who objected to everything on principle, and two elderly ladies who had come in for a warm. Stephen tried desperately to whip up some enthusiasm, reading lengthy extracts from jargon-filled correspondence with the ministries but, when Chrissie served coffee and biscuits at nine o'clock, it was obvious that he was flogging a dead horse.

'Miss Hallows would turn in her grave,' Colonel Brittan intoned, helping himself to three ginger-snaps. 'But I think these Ministry Johnnies have got us licked. When I remember how I used to shoot and fish and follow the hounds along that valley as a boy . . . '

Selena forebear to mention that the present road had curtailed any shooting and fishing for twenty years, and there had been no hunt for over forty. Or that Miss Hallows had been fully aware of the plan for the road before her death and raised no objection. Instead she smiled sympathetically at the old man, who squeezed her hand in response and seemed to cheer up considerably, perhaps remembering other pursuits he had enjoyed long ago in the valley.

After a while, Stephen disconsolately gathered up his papers. They dropped Chrissie home, then Stephen strolled back to Cloudhallows with Selena. He seemed lost in thought and let her go in alone without protest.

★ ★ ★

The next evening Mark again arrived unexpectedly. By now Selena had stopped trying to deny to herself that she eagerly awaited his visits. It was a wild night with black clouds scudding across the sky and rain beating down in the squally wind but, inside, a bright fire blazed in the sitting room hearth and a lamp glowed softly on the table near it.

Mark had brought down some crates of wine and he carried these into the house, his raincoat flung over his shoulders, while Selena placed the whisky and sherry decanters on the table.

He took off his coat and settled into an armchair by the fire, and at once some of the strain seemed to go out of his eyes. 'This is a lovely room to relax in after a hectic week.' He took the whisky which she poured for him. 'Thank you. I've brought a few wines down from town. I'd like to build up a small cellar here.'

'The part of the old buttery that is left makes a very good wine cellar.'

'Perfect. Now, what about my guests? Is Mrs. Hardy prepared to cook for them?'

'Well, she's been in a great state all week, torn both ways, but I think she's perfectly capable unless you want something really elaborate.'

'Oh, no. I thought a light lunch. Salmon, salads, something like that, and perhaps roast beef for dinner.'

'I'm sure she's up to that. I'll ask her to put a couple of menus together.

What about supplies?'

'If you'll give me the names of the best suppliers in Tivenham, I'll open accounts there. A wine merchant, too, if there's a decent one. It will save me bringing everything from town.'

Tivenham did still have a few excellent long-established stores and Selena discussed their rival merits comfortably with Mark, while the wind rose to a howl around the house and the old timbers creaked.

As Mark put a couple of logs on the fire, Selena glanced at the window. 'It's a pity you have to go,' she said unthinkingly. Then her hand flew to her mouth. 'I meant, it's such a dreadful night.'

He turned from the fire, dusting off his hands, and looked at her. Her slender figure in a soft green wool dress was curled in the big chair. The fire illuminated her heart-shaped face and deepened the copper shine of her hair.

Against all his better judgment he heard himself saying, 'I wish I could stay. And I do mean it.'

There was a silence. Selena heard the quiet tick of the old clock and the crackle of the newly-caught logs. She could think of nothing she might safely say. Then Mark resumed his seat and renewed their drinks.

'Tell me about your husband.'

'As I told you, I married very young. I was eighteen. Michael was seven years older than I, a great charmer. He was the first man friend I had ever had and, of course, he completely swept me off my feet. He was what's known as a high-flyer, always full of hare-brained schemes for making money. But he flew too high for me — and without a safety net.'

'What broke it up? Was there someone else?'

'Oh, no. Not for either of us. It was because suddenly I couldn't respect him any more. All I could see was a future of big breaks that never arrived, and fresh starts that came to nothing, leaving him more and more resentful

117

and blaming everyone except himself.'

'And now? Is there anyone else?'

'No, not really.' She managed a light laugh. 'Still licking my wounds, I guess.'

'Yes, they go absurdly deep, don't they? I married young, too, and I suppose I could have been called a high-flyer. I was trying so hard to make a material success for my wife that, I suppose, I was away from her too much. Anyway, while I was away hustling those breaks, she was consoling herself with someone else. Several someones, in fact.'

★   ★   ★

Selena was moved by the raw pain in his voice. 'How long ago?'

'The final break was five years ago. Since then I've been careful not to get too deeply involved with anyone. Just mutually enjoyable relationships between people who know the rules of the game.'

'I don't think I could manage that,' Selena said. 'Perhaps a relationship without love is harder for women.'

'I'm not speaking of a loveless relationship,' he protested. 'There can be real affection. And some women manage it very well.'

'Women like Fiona,' Selena thought. Fiona would thrive on such a no-ties relationship, but she knew it was not for her.

She steered the conversation away from such potentially dangerous waters and they talked about Mark's plans for Cloudhallows until, at ten o'clock, he rose to leave.

'I really must go, although I find it damned hard to drag myself away.'

Selena stood up, too. 'Yes, it's a terrible night,' she said again.

'I didn't mean that.'

As in the bedroom a few days previously, they stood close together. Once again a strong pulse of tension throbbed between them and their bodies were drawn together irresistibly, but now no angry shout from Stephen disturbed them.

Mark put his hands on either side of Selena's waist, and they were like burning brands on her flesh. Slowly he pulled her into his arms.

'Stop it now,' Selena commanded herself. 'Stop it while you can still draw back.' But she wanted him too much. Her body craved what it had been deprived of for so long.

He was looking down at her, his eyes dark with desire. He lowered his head and his mouth covered hers, at first gently, then more fiercely demanding. As their mouths clung, almost desperately, together, his hands moved over her back until she was pressed against every line of his taut body. Simultaneously a shudder of excitement ran through their bonded bodies.

Selena began to struggle, pushing her fists against his chest.

Her protest took a moment to penetrate. Then he released her so suddenly that she almost stumbled. When he spoke his voice was unsteady. 'I'm sorry.'

Selena said wretchedly, 'I shouldn't have let it go so far. I'm sorry.'

The anger and frustration in his face changed smoothly to formality. He gave a slight shrug and turned away. He collected his raincoat from the hall then, with the briefest of goodnights, let himself out.

Selena's emotions after his departure were as stormy as the night. She longed to be back in his arms but, at the same time, was glad she'd had the strength to call a halt. Oh, she could fall in love with him — if she hadn't already — utterly and completely, as she had never expected to again. But he had spelt out his own philosophy to her, clearly and frankly, only a short time before. He was a man who wanted a relationship with strict limitations on its extent, between people who knew the rules of the game. And such rules, where one withheld full and total commitment, weren't ones she was capable of subscribing to.

What would happen when she saw

him next? she wondered. Would there be embarrassment on his part? Probably not. He was a man of the world. He had thought she was ripe for taking — which she had demonstrated was true, she groaned inwardly. He had made a try and been repulsed, but she was pretty sure he would take it in his stride.

⋆ ⋆ ⋆

As it turned out, she didn't see him at all for the next few days. All arrangements for the guest weekend were dealt with by telephone, either by Mark's secretary or Fiona. By the Friday morning before the guests were due to arrive, everything was smoothly in hand.

Only Mrs. Hardy continued to fret, until Selena, who was getting a little irritated, said firmly, 'Mrs. Hardy, you've made these dishes scores of times before, and they're always fine so, for goodness' sake, stop worrying.'

'Oh, do you think so, dear? You don't think a few extra little touches?'

'I should leave well alone. Do things just as you usually do.'

'I'll be glad when it's over. It's keeping me awake nights worrying about it.'

'That's just silly. Come in early tomorrow and give yourself plenty of time.'

'Yes, I will. I thought I'd come in about five. If they're to eat at eight o'clock, that should be ample time. I've cancelled going to see my daughter this weekend. You will give me a hand, won't you, Selena?'

'Well, I did intend to go out. I don't want to eat with them and I'd rather not wait on them. But I'll help in the kitchen if you really think it's necessary.'

'As if I'd let you wait on that Fiona!' Mrs. Hardy was outraged. 'I would welcome a bit of help in the kitchen, though.' She was finally dispatched, claiming unconvincingly that the worry of it all had caused her to lose weight.

When Selena had finished picking at a scanty lunch, she went upstairs to put the finishing touches to the four guest rooms. She hadn't been able to bring herself to consider whether Mark and Fiona would be sharing but, even if they usually did, they would presumably observe the proprieties in front of their guests.

That done, she went outside into the garden to see what flowers were available. The brief spring weather had passed and there was a very sparse showing. Unless she could get to Tivenham to buy some, the blooms were going to have to be spread very thin.

She had just got back indoors, taken off her muddy shoes and plucked a couple of dead leaves from her hair, when she heard Mark's car in the lane. Her heart gave a lurch. She dreaded seeing him, yet it was what she had been longing for. She flew to the front door and opened it. Fiona and Mark stood together on the step, Fiona almost as tall as he, and looking utterly sure of her place at his side.

Selena felt her smile of welcome fading and jacked it back into position. 'Hello,' she said warmly. 'Come in.'

She stepped aside, feeling small and dowdy in her old sweater and skirt and without shoes. She hastily pushed her feet into sneakers. 'I've been out in the garden,' she said apologetically. 'Would you like some tea or coffee?'

'No, we can't stay long,' said Mark, looking uncomfortable. He avoided Selena's eyes and said to Fiona, 'Doesn't the house look beautiful?'

Fiona glanced around briefly. 'It looks OK, but you know what I feel about the place, darling. There are just no facilities. What on earth are people going to do?'

'They're only going to be here for two days, Fiona. They hardly need a packed agenda.'

'Well, not this pair, perhaps, but what about when Tim comes down, or Jeremy?'

'There's a golf course quite near,' Selena put in. 'And fishing, and some nice walks.'

'Walks!' Fiona looked at Selena pityingly. She glanced through the window to the back garden. 'I think we might just squeeze a tennis court in there.'

'No!' The word had burst from Selena. 'You can't do that.'

'Why ever not?'

'Because it's a very old garden, and it matches the house. A tennis court would just be wrong.'

'It's hardly any business of yours, is it?'

Her cheeks burning crimson, Selena realised the truth of Fiona's statement, but she couldn't stop herself. 'If Mr. Denning had wanted a house with tennis courts and saunas and — and helicopter pads, that's what he should have bought!'

'My point exactly,' Fiona rejoined languidly.

* * *

Mark, too, now seemed to be losing his composure. 'Well, I bought Cloud-hallows and what I do with it is my concern. Meanwhile, we just wanted to let you know of a change of plan, Selena. Fiona has offered to cook this weekend, so we won't need Mrs. Hardy.'

Selena drew a steadying breath against a new tide of anger. 'Mrs. Hardy expects to come in tomorrow night.'

'Then pay her anyway.'

'That's not the point. She's been worrying about it all week. She's worked out menus. She cancelled a visit to her daughter — '

'Well, honestly, darling — ' Fiona's drawl was scornful — 'we weren't to know that cooking a couple of meals was to be such a big production for the woman. The fact is these people are rather important and they should be given something a little bit special.'

'What about the food that's been ordered?'

'Put it in the freezer. I'll be bringing what I need from town. So you'll give her a ring, will you?'

'She isn't on the phone. I'll call and let her know.'

'And apologise from me,' Mark said. His eyes sought Selena's, but she avoided his glance. Fiona had gone back outside and he followed her, turning his raincoat collar up against the sleety wind. 'Pity the weather has turned so cold. Keep the house nice and warm, Selena. We'll be arriving — when, Fiona?'

'Say six o'clock. That should give me enough time. Will you be joining us for dinner, Selena?'

'Thank you, no,' Selena said shortly. 'I have a date.'

Fiona gave a dismissive shrug. As they walked to the car, she linked an arm in Mark's.

They drove away and Selena stood fuming. What an awful woman, she thought, to put Mrs. Hardy through all that for nothing, just so that she could show off her own prowess.

She decided not to waste any time in informing Mrs. Hardy, and put on her overcoat and knitted cap and set off briskly for her cottage. Mrs. Hardy was pleased to see her unexpected visitor and even more delighted to be let off the weekend's cooking, so that Selena began to regret her own behaviour over it in front of Mark and Fiona. Mrs. Hardy produced tea and biscuits and they spent an enjoyable half-hour criticising Fiona's whims and caprices and character in general.

On her way home through the village, Selena called at the Tremars. They had just finished tea and Selena joined Chrissie who was washing up the dishes in the kitchen.

She picked up a tea towel and started to dry. 'Chrissie, can I throw myself on your hospitality tomorrow night? I need a bolt hole. I could drive to the cinema, but I really don't fancy it.'

'Why, what's up?' Chrissie pounced eagerly. 'Aren't you invited to the feast?'

'That's just it. I am, but I'd prefer not to go. The fair Fiona has decided, at the last moment, that she's going to cook dinner.'

'And you don't want to have to admire her efforts? You can't avoid her for the whole weekend.'

'I know I can't, but the darned woman is so infuriating. Mrs. Hardy has been sweating over this all week, planning menus, ordering food, and now Fiona changes her mind. Not that Mrs. Hardy was worried, as a matter of fact. She was far less annoyed than I was.'

'This Fiona seems to have Mark Denning eating out of her hand.' Chrissie could be relied on to say the most unsettling thing. 'But certainly you're welcome to take pot luck with us,' she added.

'We'll go out somewhere,' said Stephen, who had drifted in from the dining room. 'We haven't had a meal out for a long time. How about it?'

'Lovely idea!' Chrissie glowed. 'What

about the Montpelier? I hear it's very good now.'

*　*　*

There was an embarrassed silence as Chrissie and Selena realised from Stephen's expression that the invitation had been intended for Selena alone. Then he swiftly rallied. 'All right by me. I'll ring and see if they have a table.'

He left the kitchen promptly and the two girls cleared away the dishes in a lengthening silence until he returned. 'No luck at the Montpelier. What about the Post House? Or the Bull?'

'I've been thinking,' Chrissie said. 'Why don't you just take Selena? Three's an awkward number and I've got a lot to do here.'

There was an immediate outcry of protest, merely token from Stephen, but sincere from Selena. Finally it was decided that Selena should come at about five the following evening and they would take a chance on getting a pub meal.

As Stephen walked Selena back to Cloudhallows, he let out his breath. 'Phew, that was a sticky moment. I thought we were going to be lumbered with Chris for the evening.'

'I don't in the least mind her coming. In fact, it would be a nice change for her. She doesn't get out much.'

'I take her out for a meal occasionally. But, you know — ' He hesitated. 'It's a bit awkward. She gets the wrong impression.'

Selena sighed. As a poet once said, Never the time and the place and the loved one, altogether. Tomorrow night Chris would yearn to be in her place, while she would be longing to be with Mark. And Fiona? Fiona, you could be sure, would be exactly where she wanted to be.

★   ★   ★

The next morning Mrs. Hardy had decided to be offended. She went about her chores in a sniffy silence, while

Selena put the finishing touches to the house. She opened the bathroom windows, as the still-tacky primrose paint smelt strongly, but otherwise turned up all the heating. She laid fires ready in the hall and sitting room, put reading matter and water carafes into the bedrooms, and turned down the beds.

After lunch, she picked what flowers she could find in the garden and dispersed them as best she could round the house. Then she closed the bathroom windows and lit the fires. She was changing for her date with Stephen when Chrissie arrived, just before five o'clock, her arms full of daffodils and irises, cherry blossom and forsythia.

Her face was as scarlet as her anorak. 'Gosh, it's freezing outside! I thought I'd bring you these. Our garden is always ahead of Cloudhallows.'

'Oh, thank you, Chrissie! That's wonderful. It's very kind of you. I was just thinking my flowers looked a bit few and far between. If you can wait while I arrange them, I'll walk back with you.'

'I've got a couple of calls to make before I go home.'

'Well, thanks again.'

Chris dashed out the back door as though embarrassed by her kindly gesture, and Selena quickly arranged the extra flowers.

She went back upstairs and continued her dressing, in a flattering dress of rose-coloured silk jersey topped by a loose jacket of cream raw silk, both relics of more glamorous days with Michael. She slipped a warm coat over them, checked the house for the last time, locked the doors, and dashed through the icy rain to her car. She arrived at the Tremars' house to find Stephen alone.

He kissed her warmly as he took off her coat. 'You look gorgeous! Chrissie will be back soon. She went up to Tipcroft with a prescription.'

'Yes, she called on me.'

'She did?' Stephen looked apprehensive.

134

'Yes, she brought me some of your flowers.'

'That was decent of her. Would you like some tea or something?'

'Just a cup of tea. I'm saving my appetite.'

Stephen made a tray of tea and they had just settled down before the fire in the almost-dark sitting room, when Chrissie breezed in, switching on the lights.

'What are you sitting in the dark for? Oh, good, tea! I'm ready for it after toiling up that hill.' She poured herself a cup of tea and crashed down into a chair. 'What time are the visitors arriving, Selena?'

'About six-thirty, I think. Fiona is coming a bit earlier to get things going.'

They sat around talking in a desultory fashion, until Chrissie announced, 'Well, some of us have to fend for themselves and I'm starving. I'm going to get something to eat.'

She started to cook an enormous mixed grill and, after a few minutes, Selena and Stephen left. It was a little early, but they didn't feel inclined to sit around while Chris ate her solitary meal.

They drove through country lanes until they found a pretty pub where they talked over drinks before ordering their meals. All the while, Selena's mind was half-engaged with how things were going at Cloudhallows. She felt guiltily aware of using Stephen, and set herself the tricky task of being attentive and appreciative without giving him too much romantic encouragement.

* * *

It wasn't easy. At the least warmth in her voice, or smile, he leaned closer and reached for her hand and, before long, he was proposing marriage once again.

'Please, Stephen,' Selena protested. 'I asked you not to talk about marriage.'

'I'm sorry. But it's so hard when we're together.'

'Maybe we shouldn't be together. I shouldn't have thrown myself on you tonight. All I had in mind was an evening at home with both of you.'

'I'm sorry,' Stephen said again. 'It's wonderful to be with you and I'm messing it up.' Obediently he turned to safer subjects, and they were drinking a final nightcap, near the big log fire, before he said, 'Can I just ask, Selena, how long you intend to stay at Cloudhallows? I mean — ' His voice grew querulous. 'It's an odd situation, you must admit. Just what is your position there?'

Selena considered his question. 'My position is a sort of caretaker, I suppose, with a dash of housekeeper thrown in. I don't know how 'odd' it is, but I expect to be out of it soon.'

Stephen's face radiated satisfaction. 'I'm very glad to hear it. I wouldn't like you to get yourself talked about. You know what village people are.'

'I'm not concerned with getting myself talked about, but I don't have enough to do and I feel that — that I could be in the way.'

'You mean when Denning and the Sheridan woman are in residence? Yes, I can see that could be uncomfortable. I don't imagine they need a chaperone.'

Selena winced. 'No, I don't expect they do.' She glanced at her watch. 'It's nearly eleven, Stephen. We should be getting back.'

They finished their drinks and drove slowly back through the winding lanes to Cloudhallows. They kissed goodnight in the car and Selena got out. Glancing up at the house, she was relieved to see that it was in darkness. She unlocked the front door and slipped quietly into the hall. As she did so, the lights came on and she saw Mark silhouetted in the sitting room doorway. She was about to ask him how his evening had gone when the look on his face stopped her. It was white with rage and it was directed at her. His voice, cold and clipped, said, 'I trust you had a good evening?'

'Very, thank you.' She looked at him nervously. 'Did yours go well?'

'It wasn't a total disaster — you'll be sorry to hear!'

5

For a moment Selena thought she had misheard him, but there was no mistaking the expression on his face. Her next thought was that he must be drunk.

She said, 'What did you say?'

'You heard what I said. But come inside. You've got rid of your lap-dog, I presume?'

'Do you mean Stephen?'

'That's the spaniel-eyed vet, isn't it? Is that what this is about? Because I wouldn't join in his half-baked protest? Or are you both still sore because I got Cloudhallows, and not you?'

'What are you talking about?' Selena stared at him, utterly bewildered, 'What am I supposed to have done?'

'Don't try to soften me up with your big-eyed innocence! Why don't you take your coat off? Is the house too cold?'

Selena looked around desperately for a clue. The house still appeared charming, with the sheaves of spring flowers and the log fire dying down to a pile of whispering ashes. She said doubtfully, 'It's not very warm. Did I forget to close the bathroom windows?' It seemed an incredible outburst for such a trivial oversight. 'I remember I opened them because the paint wasn't quite dry.'

'Opened the bathroom windows! You don't believe in such half measures. Every window in the house was wide open and — in case that wasn't enough to do the trick — the heating had been switched off, too.'

She continued to stare at him. 'It's not true!'

'I asked you to do one thing for me, to see that the house was warm and comfortable. Hardly onerous duties, I think you'll agree.'

'But it was, it was! All the windows were closed. The heating was on high. I lit two fires. If anything, it was too warm.'

'You had lit fires, I agree. But the heating was off and Fiona says all the windows were open. When I arrived with my guests the house was still icy.'

'You didn't come with Fiona?'

'No, we arrived about half-an-hour after her.'

'Then she did it!' Selena exclaimed. 'She must have done. When I left, just after five o'clock, the heating was on and the windows were closed.'

His expression grew contemptuous. 'Why on earth would Fiona do it? She wanted the evening to be a success. She knew it was important to me. But you've been dragging your heels over my plans from the start.'

'That's not true!' Selena protested, close to tears now. 'Perhaps, at the beginning, I had doubts about what you wanted to do, but since then you can't say I haven't collaborated.'

Mark turned and kicked at one of the dying logs in exasperation. He raked a hand through his hair. 'Oh, get your coat off, for heaven's sake!' He turned back to her, standing in front of him obediently in her rose-coloured dress, her jacket in her hands. He half-snatched the coat from her. 'Sit down!'

* * *

Selena slid into an armchair and looked up at him fearfully. She thought he had conceded the truth of her words but, after a moment, he said, 'You gave every appearance of collaborating, to the full extent of your considerable charms! Was it the classic attack on two fronts? Tremar having failed to bore me to death, you soften me up with your feminine wiles. He must be keen on his road protest to let you loose on me the way he did. It nearly went further than he intended.'

Sickened by his jibe, Selena shook her head wearily. 'Stephen had nothing to do with it. I locked up here and went straight to his house. We were together all evening.'

'Who else has a key?'

'You have a front door key. Mrs. Hardy has one to the back door. I have one of each.'

'I gave my key to Fiona. What about Mrs. Hardy?'

'What about her?'

'You seemed to think she'd resent the change of plans over the cooking. Would she play this sort of trick?'

Selena looked at him scornfully. 'That's ridiculous. Firstly, she simply isn't that sort of person. As it turned out she was heartily relieved to get out of the cooking. Secondly, nothing on this earth would have induced her to leave her fireside and TV and toil up here on an evening like this.'

There was a pause. Selena said, 'Look, suppose Fiona turned off the heating accidentally. Pushed the wrong switch. She could have made up the story to cover herself.'

'The windows had certainly been open. The carpets were soaked with sleet beneath them. And the house had been cold for much longer than the half-hour between our arrivals. In any case, she wouldn't do such a stupid thing.'

'Oh, no!' Selena exploded childishly. 'She's a paragon of efficiency!'

He looked at her sharply. 'So that's it? You're jealous of her.'

Selena was aware that she was on quicksand. Her voice, when it came, was shaky. 'Why should I be jealous of her?'

'You can't deny that she's got her act together rather better than you have. You were afraid of life with your high-risk husband, so you hid yourself away down here. You haven't the guts to — to acknowledge your own needs.' His voice faltered. After a moment, he said, 'I realise you were annoyed over the change of plan yesterday.'

'I was annoyed,' Selena said shortly. 'I wasn't demented.'

'What about that cousin of Tremar's? It seems to me she would do a lot to further his cause.'

'Chrissie?' Whatever tricks Chrissie

might resort to, breaking up a budding romance between Selena and another man was the last thing she would want, although that was something she couldn't spell out to Mark. 'She'd be the last person.'

'Then it must remain a mystery?'

'It is to me. I only hope your guests being a little chilly didn't spoil the impression you wished to make.'

'I wasn't interested in making an impression, but one of my guests is elderly and not in good health.'

Selena felt small, as no doubt he had intended. 'Well,' she said feebly, 'the house is warm now.'

'Yes, Fiona built up the fires and found an oil heater to supplement them and soon got things comfortable.'

'Bully for Fiona!' Selena stood up. 'I'm very tired. If you've no objection, I'm going to bed. Under the circumtances, I shall move out as soon as possible.'

'That might be best.'

She brushed past him and ran up the

stairs to her room. One small lamp burned on the landing and all was quiet. She was trembling with distress and anger. How could Fiona have played such a malicious trick? For she was convinced it was Fiona's doing. She had resented Selena's presence at Cloudhallows from the start. Perhaps it was understandable, Selena thought. Perhaps she had been insensitive, hanging on here. Well, that would end soon. All she had to do was get through this ghastly weekend.

She stripped off her dress, put on her dressing-gown and, after a cautious peep round the door, sneaked along to the bathroom. She was as quick and quiet as possible, and was relieved to get back to her room without encountering anyone.

*　*　*

The night was sheer misery. Sleep was out of the question as the scene with Mark replayed itself over and over. She

146

must have dozed off just before dawn, because she woke at eight, having forgotten for a moment the events of the night until they rolled over her in horrible vividness.

Rallying her spirits, she sped to the bathroom and quickly showered. Then she shot down to the kitchen. It was deserted. She made herself a pot of tea and some toast and returned with it to her room. As she tiptoed past the closed doors on the landing, she couldn't help wondering where Mark and Fiona were sleeping.

She got into bed with the breakfast tray but, though the tea was welcome, the toast stuck like cottonwool in her throat. Finally she gave up and, putting the tray aside, slid down under the bedclothes, listening for sounds of movement in the house.

She heard Mark's footsteps first then, when he had gone downstairs, the slower tread of an older man. He coughed a good deal and it was evident that the open windows had done him no good at all. He was followed by the heavier tread of another man then, finally, Selena heard the clack of Fiona's high-heeled mules.

At ten o'clock Selena decided she simply couldn't skulk upstairs all day. She was, after all, the injured party. She put on her blue tweed slacks and a soft blue mohair sweater, applied a little make-up, brushed her hair, and descended the stairs.

There was a clatter of dishes being washed in the kitchen, but the three men were seated in the hall. They all rose as Selena entered. She wondered how Mark had accounted for the strange events of the previous night, but he introduced her to his visitors with formal courtesy.

'Selena, may I present Dr. David Gershon and Robert Halliday?'

Mr. Halliday was much what she had been expecting. Fiftyish, sleek and well-fed looking, and expensively dressed in the city man's idea of country-wear. Gershon, on the other hand, was elderly and looked frail, with lines deeply etched on his face.

Selena found herself saying, 'I'm terribly sorry that there was some misunderstanding over the heating last night.'

Gershon smiled. 'Don't think of it! I'm not quite the hot-house plant that Mark here, seems to imagine. You are too young to remember, dear lady, but people did manage to survive before the advent of central heating.'

'Fiona soon got things warmed up, and her wonderful meal erased any memories,' Halliday put in.

★   ★   ★

Fiona, hearing Selena's arrival, had hastened into the hall, an expression of gleeful anticipation on her face.

'Yes, it was unfortunate, but no harm done,' Mark said smoothly. 'A matter of the paint on some window frames still being wet.'

Selena was amused to see Fiona's

quickly concealed look of irritation.

'What an upheaval it is, the renovation of an old house,' Gershon said. 'One must be so careful not to spoil its original character. This one has been preserved beautifully.' Selena sat down beside the old man, while he began to question her about the history of Cloudhallows.

Fiona seemed more drawn to the prosperous-looking Mr. Halliday, who ogled her as she perched on the arm of his chair.

After a while, Selena said, 'Does anyone want coffee?'

They all acquiesced and she was setting the cups out on a tray when Mark followed her into the kitchen.

'I thought we might drive to Oxford for lunch,' he said.

Selena nodded. Mark gazed out over the garden, rocking on his heels and apparently searching for something further to say.

Finally, indicating the tray of cups, he settled for, 'Shall I take those in?'

Selena thanked him coolly and followed a moment later with the coffee and cream.

With the refreshments, the company grew even more relaxed. Robert Halliday turned his heavy charm on Selena, to Fiona's obvious annoyance. Mark talked mainly to Dr. Gershon but, once or twice, Selena caught his eyes on her in quiet speculation.

Eventually, the three men and Fiona left for their lunch trip, Halliday having made a determined effort to persuade Selena to join them.

★   ★   ★

When they had gone she heaved a sigh of relief. The morning had passed much more agreeably than she had dared hope. She washed up the coffee cups, then went upstairs to the bedrooms. Four rooms seemed to have been used and Fiona's, after only one night, was chaotically untidy. She made the beds and tidied up, cleaned the bathrooms,

151

then prepared an omelette for her own lunch. Mid-afternoon found her feeling a little tense, and she decided to do some baking, always good therapy for her. For the next hour she turned out scones, shortbread and a featherlight sponge.

She was well-pleased with her efforts, when at four o'clock, the visitors made a noisy entrance, Robert Halliday, at least, having obviously wined — as well as lunched — very well.

He stamped into the kitchen, sniffing appreciatively. 'What a welcome! This is the life!'

Fiona, close behind him, stretched a smile. 'Why, Selena, how clever of you. I had no idea you could cook.'

Selena affected to notice her much-prized efforts. 'Oh, those!' she said casually. 'Just a few scones and biscuits. I don't really call myself a cook.'

Mark smiled his appreciation. 'Thank you, Selena. This was good of you.'

Selena made tea while the others took off their outdoor clothes, then wheeled the laden trolley into the hall, where she had made up a big fire.

Fiona stretched out her shapely hands to the blaze. 'Well, I must say, this is an improvement on last night!'

Selena's stomach lurched, but Fiona's gambit was totally ignored. The three men tucked into Selena's baking so heartily that Fiona protested sharply that they wouldn't be able to eat their dinner.

At six-thirty, Fiona moved to the kitchen to start preparing dinner and Selena went to assist in such humble tasks as preparing vegetables. She couldn't help admiring the other girl's confident expertise, and told her so. They worked together in an apparent truce until everything could be left for a short while, then went upstairs to shower and change.

★   ★   ★

Selena put on a dramatically-cut dress of sage-green jersey, which showed off her figure to perfection. Fiona, when she emerged from her bedroom, was also wearing green, but a dramatic emerald shade, and her hair was piled up on her head.

Mark was pouring drinks for his guests. All three men looked up in admiration as the girls descended the stairs.

Robert Halliday spoke first. 'Charming! Quite charming, ladies!'

Dr. Gershon smiled his sweet smile. 'You both look delightful, my dears.'

Mark said nothing, but got drinks for the two girls and, after a few minutes, Fiona returned to the kitchen to put the finishing touches to the meal.

The dinner was superb and conversation flowed easily. Seated between Robert Halliday and Dr. Gershon, Selena found, to her surprise, that she was enjoying herself. Mark, seated across the table, said little to her, but seemed unable to take his eyes off her.

As Fiona had said, it was certainly an improvement on the previous night.

After her disturbed night, and the wine she had drunk, Selena was sleepy and in a much happier frame of mind. Nevertheless, as she quickly prepared for bed, she was still determined to leave Cloudhallows at the first opportunity.

★　★　★

The next morning she rose early and got her own breakfast, then prepared some for the others as they drifted downstairs. After breakfast, they said goodbye to Selena, Robert Halliday presenting her with a large box of chocolates he had somehow acquired.

While the others went out to the cars, Mark lingered behind. Standing inside the front door with Selena, he asked her stiffly, 'Won't you consider staying?'

She looked at him in surprise. 'Why should you want me here? You don't trust me.'

He didn't refute it. 'Can't we forget it? Call it some sort of silly mix-up?'

'No,' she said. 'No, it wasn't that.'

Fiona called impatiently from the car. Mark hesitated, then touched Selena awkwardly on the arm. 'I hope you'll let me know your plans.'

Selena stood in the doorway watching them disappear out of sight down the lane, then turned back inside. There was a painful knot of tears in her throat at Mark's leaving in this way, alienated and mistrusting, after the closeness they had begun to enjoy. But that very closeness had gone too far, she thought, remembering her near-surrender on the evening when he had brought the wine. Better in every way that she should get out while she was still relatively unscathed.

She had little time to mope. In ten minutes Mrs. Hardy arrived, agog for a blow-by-blow account of the entire weekend. Selena told her everything that had transpired, only omitting the business of the opened windows.

'Good cook, is she, that Fiona?' Mrs. Hardy enquired wistfully at the end of the recital.

'Very good.'

When Mrs. Hardy at last got down to her chores, Selena put on her jacket, got out the car, and drove into Tivenham. It was still very cold with occasional flurries of snow in the air. She had set out with no clear plan of what she was going to do but, as she approached the town, she suddenly had an idea. Miss Parry.

Miss Parry had been head teacher of the infant school where Selena's father headed the junior department for as long as she could remember. She had received Selena herself into school when she was just five years old. She had retired seven years ago to keep house for an older sister who, Selena had heard, had recently died. Miss Parry knew everybody in Tivenham. If she didn't want a boarder herself, she would certainly know someone who did.

It didn't take Selena long to locate the tall, terraced house overlooking the river. Miss Parry was so delighted to see her that Selena was consumed with guilt over not visiting before.

When Selena had filled her in on what she had been doing since her father died, Miss Parry said, 'Yes, I knew Miss Hallows slightly. A delightful woman. So, now you will be setting off into the world again?'

'Actually, I'm looking for somewhere to live, Miss Parry. I wondered if you knew of anywhere in Tivenham?'

'Isn't Tivenham a bit of a backwater, my dear? You used to be the boldest spirit in my school. You haven't lost your zest for life, I trust?'

Selena looked into shrewd blue eyes. 'It's only temporarily, while I decide what to do.'

'Haven't you just had two years to decide what to do? But it's nothing to do with me. If you really want to get stuck with another old lady, I'd be more than happy for you to have my top floor.

'I was just about to advertise the rooms,' Miss Parry explained as they

158

went upstairs. 'So your arrival was timely. I would far rather have you here than a stranger.' She pushed open two doors on the bright, newly-painted landing. 'I've had them redecorated, and renewed the furnishings.'

★   ★   ★

The rooms were delightful, large and high-ceilinged, and freshly decorated with cream paint. They were furnished as a bedroom and a sitting room, with an attractive mixture of good old pieces and some new ones that Miss Parry had added. Big windows overlooked the full, swift river that flowed behind trees across the road, giving a fluid, translucent light to the rooms.

The kitchen was on the ground floor, and the bathroom on the first floor. Miss Parry apologised for this, but Selena was unconcerned.

'It's a gorgeous flat!' she exclaimed, in genuine pleasure. 'I'd love to take it, if I may?'

'You're more than welcome, my dear. When would you like to move in?'

'It won't take me long to get my things together. Would Friday morning be all right?'

'That will be fine, Selena. I'll expect you then.'

Miss Parry named a rent which seemed far too low then, with mixed feelings, Selena drove back to Fairbridge. She was glad that she had made a definite break with Cloudhallows and its now distressing circumstances, yet sad to be leaving behind the happiness she had known there in the past, and the glimpsed, much greater joy that might have been.

It was long past lunchtime when she got back to the house, and Mrs. Hardy had left. She made herself a snack and took tea out to the workmen engaged on the new garage. After lunch she tried to contact Mark, to let him know that she would be leaving, but he was not available and she left the message with a secretary. Stephen must be told, too, but there was no hurry for that.

She went over the house, slowly gathering her belongings together, pausing to recall the memory each item conjured up. It was dark before she had deposited everything in her room. She packed her clothes, apart from what she would need for a couple of days, into her case, but the odd shapes and sizes of shoes and books would need another box. She had used all that she could find at Cloudhallows, but Stephen would be sure to have something suitable in his dispensary.

She went to the study and tidied away her notes in the bureau, and piled up the books ready for return to the library. She was on her way to the kitchen to make a pot of tea, when she was startled by a loud insistent knocking at the front door.

Her heart pounded. It could only be Mark. Stephen rarely called without first phoning. What could have brought him? Surely not her message to his office. She was hurrying to the door when it struck her that it was now Mark's custom to knock quietly and then let himself in.

Suddenly apprehensive, she stopped, gazing at the door with foreboding. The loud knocking came again and slowly she reached out and unlatched the door.

On the doorstep stood a tall man wearing a raincoat, the collar turned up against the cold wind. Selena peered at him in the dim light from the hall. Then her heart gave a wild lurch.

'Michael?' she whispered wonderingly.

6

'Hello, Selena,' he said.

She continued to stare at him and he smiled the lop-sided smile that had once been guaranteed to turn her legs to jelly.

'Well, aren't you going to ask me in? It's perishing out here.'

'I'm sorry.' Somehow the words were forced from her stiff lips. She stepped back into the hall and he followed her in. He took off his raincoat, while his eyes ranged round the hall, assessing it.

'You took some tracking down,' he complained. 'What on earth are you doing in this back-of-beyond?'

'Why did you want to track me down?'

'Old times' sake, darling. And glad I am that I found you, because you're even more beautiful than I remembered.'

Before Selena could move, he had

163

reached out and pulled her to him. His mouth came slowly down on hers with confidence and he kissed her long and hard.

Pressed against his muscular body, Selena waited for the old magic to wreak its havoc. Oh, there was some. She had been loveless for a long time and Michael was a master, but he wasn't irresistible, not by a very long way. And part of its failure to work was Michael's arrogant certainty that it would.

She waited for the kiss to end and drew back, only a little disturbed.

He looked at her, faintly puzzled. 'I must have been an idiot — '

'So it has been said. I still don't understand why you are here, and spare me the blarney, please. I would hope we've both grown out of that.'

He shrugged slightly. 'I happened to be passing through Tivenham. I thought I must look you up, but when I went to your father's house, you were no longer there.'

'My father died.'

'Yes, they told me. I'm sorry.'

'Well, now that you're here, would you like a drink, or some coffee?'

'Coffee would be great.'

Selena led the way into the kitchen. 'I'll make some sandwiches. I haven't eaten since lunchtime.'

'Fine, fine.' He was taking an inventory of the kitchen now, putting a price tag on everything, as he always did.

'It's a nice house,' he said, 'although scarcely your scene, I'd have thought.'

'You'd have no idea of my scene, Michael,' she said calmly.

'So — what are you doing here? Did you buy the place?'

'No, I've been working here. Actually, I'm leaving in a couple of days. I'm moving back to Tivenham.'

'Have you bought a house there?'

'No, I've just taken a flat for the time being.'

She made the coffee and carried the tray through to the sitting room. She set the tray down on the table and poked up the fire in the hearth. As she poured their coffee, she reflected on the unlikely scene. Never had she expected to be doing this with Michael again.

★ ★ ★

He accepted the coffee and leant back in his chair almost wearily. There was something slightly down-at-heel about him. Although the big, near-diamond, cufflinks still flashed, Selena recognised his well-pressed suit as five-years-old, and his shoes were not the quality he once would have worn.

'Life seems to be treating you well, Selena. You look positively blooming.'

She smiled slightly. 'Country air.'

'No, it's more than that.' He looked at her intently. 'You haven't remarried, have you?'

'No. I didn't think our venture was any great advertisement for the married state.'

'Oh, come on! We had some great

times. I remember them as the best in my life. But there is a man, isn't there?'

'Damn you, Michael Brent,' Selena thought. 'You could always read me like a book.'

'No,' she said firmly. 'There's no one. I'm having a sabbatical.'

He seemed to relax at her words. He picked up a sandwich and took a large bite, almost as though he hadn't eaten all day. 'What a waste! So, tell me all. What have you been doing with yourself these past three years?'

Selena found herself telling him. It was one of Michael's virtues that he was an excellent listener. She even began to enjoy his company as he listened, with sympathetic comments, to her account of her father's last year and her two years with Miss Hallows. She didn't mention Mark, simply saying that the house had been sold on Miss Hallows' death and that she was now moving out.

'I found a flat this morning,' she finished. 'With Miss Parry, my old schoolteacher. I think I shall be happy there. And you, Michael? What have you been doing?'

'Oh, this and that,' he said vaguely. 'I'm on to a very good thing at the moment. A really first-rate opportunity. Just a matter of getting my hands on a little capital.'

'That sounds familiar.'

'Oh, no, this is something quite new for me. A friend and I are buying up old boats, restoring them, and renting them out as holiday craft.'

★ ★ ★

As far as Selena knew, Michael had no knowledge whatever of boats. She said dubiously, 'It has possibilities, as long as you make sure they're seaworthy. But I didn't mean this particular venture was familiar. I meant your looking for 'a little capital'.'

'Yes, the story of my life,' he said sombrely. 'It's held me back in everything I've attempted. You can't succeed at a single thing without backing.'

Selena sighed. It was Michael's lifelong conviction that every success story was founded on early privilege and nothing was going to shake it now.

He had finished the sandwiches and had started on Robert Halliday's chocolates when he appeared to be struck by a sudden inspiration. 'I say, Selena, you wouldn't be interested in investing, I suppose? It's an absolutely safe bet.'

Selena's first reaction was anger that she had been so slow catching on. The second was a wave of revulsion that made her feel physically sick.

She managed to say, 'What makes you think I have money to invest?'

'You sold your father's house, didn't you?'

He would have known that, of course, before he ever came to Tivenham, and, very likely, the exact sum she had got for it.

'I intend to buy a house with that money.'

'But not immediately. I suppose, in the meantime, it's safely invested in some piddling little two-per-cent?'

'A bit more than that. But 'safely' is the operative word.'

'Selena, I can't believe I'm hearing this! You used to be such a risk-taker. And, now, when we have some cash for the first time in our lives —'

To combat the anger and hurt that flooded her, Selena piled the dishes on to the tray, so that they clattered under her trembling hands.

'*My* life, Michael. It's not a matter of our lives any longer. Forget it! Not a chance,' she added, as he started to protest. 'And now, I think you'd better leave. It's getting late.'

He didn't move. He stared into the fire for a few moments, then he said, 'You've changed, Selena. You've grown hard.'

'I've grown up. Let's just say good-bye, Michael, before this gets unpleasant.'

He lifted his head and looked at her, and she saw a man stripped of charm and vitality. 'Things are a bit tough at the moment, Selena, to be honest.'

'I'm sorry, Michael, but I don't want to hear any of this. You must go.'

'I'd hoped to get a bed for the night.'

Selena was horrified. 'You can't stay here! I'll give you money for a hotel.'

'I won't get a room in Tivenham at this hour of the night.'

She saw the truth in that. 'You'll just have to drive on for a bit. Maybe in Oxford.'

'I don't have a car.'

'What? But how did you get here?'

'I took the bus to Tivenham. A guy gave me a lift to the top of the lane.'

       ★   ★   ★

For a second her heart was touched at the debonair Michael, so proud of always having the latest model of car, hitching lifts and riding buses. But only for a second.

'Michael, you simply take my breath away! Do you mean to say you came to

Tivenham to relieve me of any money I might have, without even the means to get away after?'

'It was nothing like that. It was an impulse. I just felt like seeing you again.'

'After three years?' Selena considered furiously. The thought of driving him to Tivenham and trying to book him into one of the few staid little hotels, where he would be instantly recognised as her ex-husband, was even less attractive than the alternative.

'All right,' she said ungraciously. 'You can stay tonight, but you must leave first thing in the morning. After that, I don't ever want to see you again.'

'Thanks, Selena. I'll get my bag.'

'Your bag?'

'I left it outside in the hedge.' He grinned. 'It didn't look too good, turning up on the doorstep with it!' He went outside to return a moment later with his overnight bag. She should have known that never, whatever the circumstances, would he be found without a fresh shirt.

172

He was incorrigible but, after tonight, she would be free of him. Completely free in a way she had never been quite sure of. With a sense of relief, she went upstairs and made up a bed for him in one of the spare rooms. When she came down, she got him a drink and they talked again.

At eleven o'clock, she said, 'It's been a long day, Michael. I'm going to bed.'

He stood up. 'Alone?'

'Yes, alone.'

He put his hands on her shoulders and kissed her lightly. 'Goodnight, Selena. I'm sorry if I managed to hurt you yet again. You were the best thing that ever happened to me, but I never could seem to hang on to anything worthwhile.'

Selena opened her mouth to reply, but there was too much, or too little, to say, so she simply bade him goodnight, locked up the house, and they went upstairs to bed.

★ ★ ★

The following morning she was up early to make sure that Michael was off the premises before Mrs. Hardy's arrival.

She had to steel her heart against sentiment as they ate breakfast together, a situation, in its way, as intimate as a shared bedroom. Michael was very quiet, as though he, too, had finally realised that there was nothing left between them. He managed to eat a hearty breakfast nevertheless, then followed her out to the car. They drove to Tivenham almost in silence. At the bus station, Selena pushed forty pounds, all the cash she had in the house, into his hand. He smiled his charming lop-sided smile, almost as a reflex, and disappeared inside.

Selena sat for a moment with her hands on the wheel, tears pricking her eyes. Then she swallowed hard, turned around, and headed back for Fairbridge. As she approached the village, she decided to call on Stephen. Chris was out when she arrived, but Stephen answered her request for packing cases by producing a couple of cartons from a cupboard under the stairs. He was clearly delighted that she was leaving Cloudhallows, but would still be living close at hand.

'I'm sure you're doing the right thing.' He beamed. 'What made you decide?'

'It was a spur-of-the-moment decision. No, that's not true. Mark and his guests are obviously going to be in residence more now and I could be in the way.'

'Very likely. Would you like coffee?'

'Mm, please.'

Stephen started the coffee. 'How did the weekend go?'

'Oh, fine. The guests were very pleasant. The elderly one particularly.' She had no intention of mentioning the window episode, or Michael's visit. 'I seem to be getting very secretive all of a sudden,' she thought. 'Not so long ago I would have poured out every detail at the drop of a hat.'

They were still drinking their coffee when Chris returned. She was as pleased as Stephen to hear of Selena's imminent departure, and hid it even less well. Together they promised to help her to move to Tivenham.

'They can't wait to see the back of me,' she thought ruefully, as she threaded her way through a pack of Reardons, back to Cloudhallows.

With Mrs. Hardy, however, it was a different matter. Selena's news brought a touching flood of tears and a firm pronouncement that, if Selena was leaving, she had no intention of staying on.

'But that's foolish, Mrs. Hardy,' Selena protested. 'I know you wanted to keep your job.'

'I couldn't work for that Fiona. Not if she's going to mess me about like last time. I'd rather starve!' she concluded dramatically. She packed away her tools, put on her coat and outdoor shoes, and took herself off, still sniffing.

* * *

Selena got herself some lunch, then decided to put in some work in the garden. During the warmer weather of the week before, everything had grown furiously, and there was a lot of weeding and general tidying to be done.

After tea she packed one of Stephen's boxes with her odds-and-ends and, at eight o'clock, aching painfully from her activity in the garden, she decided to take a bath.

She was towelling her hair when she heard a tap at the front door, followed by a key being turned in the lock. She froze. There was no doubting this time that it was Mark. She pulled on her towelling robe and rubbed at the steamy mirror. Her make-up-free face was flushed and her hair sprang up in damp auburn curls. She had never felt so vulnerable in her life.

'Selena,' she heard him call from the hall.

She opened the bathroom door and

came out on to the landing.

He was standing at the bottom of the staircase looking up. His eyes met hers and a succession of emotions were reflected in them. Embarrassment, attraction, desire — perhaps even something deeper.

He said, 'I'm sorry. Have I got you out of your bath?'

'No, I'd finished.' She came downstairs trying to pull the entirely adequate robe tighter about her. 'Is anything the matter?'

'A message was passed to me from my office that you were leaving in a couple of days.'

'Yes.'

His embarrassment was now obvious. 'I was passing through — ' He broke off, well aware that no one passed through Fairbridge.

After a moment, she said, 'I'm sorry, but I didn't think I'd be putting you out. I always intended to go soon, and a very nice flat has come up in the house of a friend.'

Mark couldn't take his eyes off her. There was a scented, baby-softness about her that was contradicted by a powerful womanly appeal. The urge to seize her in his arms and hold her to him almost overwhelmed him. He retreated swiftly to the hall fireplace and gave his attention to the dying fire.

He cleared his throat. 'I seem to have over-reacted, but I thought we had something between us. Some sort of relationship — ' Again his voice tailed off.

*   *   *

Never before had Selena seen him in less than complete control of himself. She slid into the armchair beside the fireplace, where only two nights previously he had berated her.

'I have no role here,' she said. 'I feel something of an intruder.'

'That's ridiculous!' He was burningly conscious of her closeness again. Her head, only inches from his thigh, so

179

disturbed him that his reaction sounded like anger. And it was a sort of anger. Anger that the self-protecting armour-plate that he had grown over the years was so near to being pierced.

'I suppose it was the business over the windows? Surely I had the right to be angry?'

'Certainly you had the right. You were angry with the wrong person, that's the trouble. I had nothing to do with it. But that's not really the reason I'm leaving. I feel I'm just marking time here. I should get on with my life.' She smiled faintly. 'You told me so yourself.'

'Does that include Stephen Tremar?' The words seemed to be forced from him.

'In some capacity, I suppose. He's a good friend.'

'And he's content with that? But it's none of my business, is it?' He kicked at a log, sending a bright shower of sparks up the vast chimney. 'Well, I don't intend to try to change your mind.'

There was a brief silence, then he

said, 'I suppose Mrs. Hardy will be leaving, too?'

'She said this morning that she intended to.'

'And Jordan?'

'Oh, I imagine he'll stay on.'

'I spoke to him the last time he was working here. He said he would stay as long as you were here.'

'Jordan said that? But he has never addressed an inessential word to me!'

At last he turned to look at her. Her face, upturned to his, was soft in the firelight, and the last cold barrier of his defence was penetrated. 'It isn't necessary. You have a magic — '

He put his arms around her and drew her to him and his words were stopped as their lips met.

Now she knew the magic that had been absent with Michael, the completeness of love and passion fused together. She slipped her arms around Mark's neck and drew him closer.

His reaction was explosive. He eased her back into the big chair, lowering himself over her. Their mouths still clung together as though they could not bear to part before they had slaked their thirsts. His body was pressed to hers, his breath harshly imperative. He slid a hand beneath her robe to sear her waiting flesh. She gasped. A quiver ran through her as her body arched helplessly to meet his.

At the last moment he drew back and looked into her eyes. 'Do you want this, my love? Are you quite sure?'

For answer she dropped her head on to his chest and he lowered her gently to the rug.

★ ★ ★

The following morning, Selena rose first. She went about her toilet, humming beneath her breath. When she looked in the mirror, the fatuous expression on her face made her smile even more broadly.

It was much warmer; suddenly spring was back to match her mood. As she opened the bathroom window a slight frown appeared on her brow. If only she could solve the mystery of the opened windows. It was such a stupid little thing, her impulse was to sweep it under the carpet, and yet it lay between them, a tiny niggling doubt.

She shrugged, pulled on her blue velour track-suit, and ran downstairs. She had just set breakfast, when Mark came into the kitchen.

Nuzzling her ear, he said, 'I was in two minds about rumpling a second bed for Mrs. Hardy's benefit.'

Selena blushed a becoming pink. 'Oh dear, I hadn't thought of that! She'll be here any minute. But no, I wouldn't want to deceive her.' She released herself from his arms. 'Do you want a cooked breakfast?'

'Certainly, I do.'

He fetched the paper from the hall while Selena cooked bacon, eggs and tomatoes for them. As they breakfast in the sunny kitchen, she thought again, as she had with Michael, what an intimate situation breakfasting together was. They had finished their meal and were on a second cup of coffee, when Mrs. Hardy arrived.

She stopped in surprise when she saw Mark at the table. 'Well, you're an early visitor, Mr. Denning.'

Mark said easily, 'I spent the night here, Mrs. Hardy.'

'Oh, that accounts for it,' Mrs. Hardy responded placidly. 'I'll get on with the bedrooms then, while you finish your breakfasts.'

She collected her tools and clattered upstairs. Mark raised an eyebrow. 'Either the significance of this has escaped her, or she is more sophisticated than I thought.'

'The former, I imagine. I'm pretty firmly linked with Stephen in her mind.'

But, ten minutes later, Mrs. Hardy had obviously made the connection. She re-entered the room, with a look of arch connivance on her face. Beaming at Mark, she extended her hand. 'I found this in the bathroom, sir. It had rolled under the mat.' In her palm lay a large diamond cufflink.

There was a long silence. Then Mark touched the bauble with a fastidious finger. 'It's not mine, Mrs. Hardy,' he said. 'It's a bit flash for my taste.'

★   ★   ★

'Perhaps it belongs to one of the gentlemen who stayed at the weekend,' Mrs. Hardy suggested, 'although I'm almost sure it wasn't there yesterday morning.'

'It's mine,' Selena said hastily. 'I sometimes wear them in a blouse. I'm sorry you don't approve of my taste, Mark!'

Mrs. Hardy looked dubious, but handed the link to Selena. She seemed to sense a tension in the air and immediately returned to the upstairs rooms.

There was another silence. The blood had drained from Selena's face. 'Why did I tell such a stupid lie,' she thought?

'Why on earth didn't I tell him about Michael?' But now was not the time. Confession after discovery rarely rings true.

Mark's face was bleak. All the new warmth had been wiped from it. He pushed back his chair and rose from the table.

Selena said, 'Where are you going?'

'Back to town.'

She indicated the glittering cufflink. 'Is it because of that? Mark, it isn't what you think.'

'You'd better return it to Stephen. It may have sentimental value.'

'It doesn't belong to Stephen.'

'Don't lie to me, Selena.'

She got up and stood facing him. 'It isn't Stephen's!'

'I'll admit it doesn't seem his style. Nor did the aftershave that I thought I smelled still hanging around in the bathroom.' Pain turned his smile into a grimace. 'No wonder Mrs. Hardy didn't turn a hair this morning!'

She drew back her arm and struck

him hard in the face. 'How dare you?'

He put his hand up to the scarlet mark on his cheek. 'You're quite right. You're perfectly free to do as you like. But it's not your morals that offend me, it's your deceit. There seemed to be an implication last night that I was the first since — '

Her pale cheeks flooded with colour. 'It was the truth.'

'Please don't lie to me. First it was the windows — '

'Oh, the damned windows!' she exploded. 'How many times do I have to tell you that *I didn't open them*! Why don't you hound that paragon, Fiona?'

'Because I know her to be trustworthy. And because she had no motive.'

'What motive am I supposed to have had?'

'That's what I couldn't understand. I couldn't believe that it was merely pique because I, and not you, had got Cloudhallows. But then I got to thinking about Stephen's fanatical opposition to the new road passing here. Cynic that I am, I couldn't quite accept that it was pure enthusiasm for the environment. So I made a visit to the county records office, and what do you think I found?

'I found that the alternative route for the new road, the useless strip along the river bank that would then be so essential, is owned by none other than Stephen Tremar. It was bought in 1938 by his father, long before our Stephen was born, but he still holds title to it and, if he can manage to nobble the Cloudhallows route, he'll certainly get a five-figure sum for it.'

Selena was staring at him, mesmerised. 'It's not true.'

★ ★ ★

Mark looked into her gold-flecked eyes. He saw the shock on her face. Could it be an act? Never before in his life had he wanted so much to believe anyone.

'You really didn't know?' His words

were somewhere between a jeer and a plea. 'You told me you had done research on the village in the records office.'

She shook her head dumbly. 'Not of such recent date. When did you find this out?'

'Yesterday morning. I intended to have it out in the open. Then when I was told you were leaving, I fell into your arms like a lovesick schoolboy and it went out of my head. What an idiot you must have thought me!'

'Mark!' His name was wrenched from her like a cry of pain.

Her voice and her expression tore at his heart, but his instinct of self-protection had been forged through years of unhappiness. He couldn't bear to face her. He crossed to the window and looked over the sunny garden.

'I do understand how vital it was for Tremar to have the owner of Cloud-hallows eating out of his hand,' he said. 'What I don't understand is why you didn't make a bigger offer for the house yourselves. It would have been worth the outlay. Couldn't you raise the cash? But, of course, John Farmer sold it over your heads, didn't he? So you had to start hatching your little schemes. First, you were delegated to soften me up — '

Some perverse cruelty that was hurting him almost as much as her drove him on, but Selena could bear to hear no more. She dropped her head into her hands and rushed from the kitchen to blunder blindly up the stairs.

If they had been alone in the house, Mark would probably have followed her, but hearing Mrs. Hardy's indignant queries on the landing, his pride won and he grabbed his coat and slammed out to his car.

Upstairs, Selena was parrying Mrs. Hardy's questions as best she could with tears streaming down her face. She heard the front door banged and the furious revving of Mark's car engine. Mrs. Hardy accepted with surprising tact that Selena didn't want to talk and let her escape to her bedroom.

In her room she collapsed on to her bed, still rumpled from their loving bodies. She buried her head in the pillow and sobbed bitterly.

Mark's accusations, following so swiftly on their night of love and discovery, had put her almost into a condition of shock. The revelation of Stephen's deceit sickened her, but she was still convinced that he had no part in opening the windows. On Saturday afternoon she had locked the doors of Cloudhallows, gone directly to his house, and spent the evening with him. Fiona, she was sure, was responsible for that spiteful act.

★   ★   ★

After a while, Selena turned on to her back, looking up at the ceiling. She wished that she could leave Cloud-hallows right away, instead of waiting two unnecessary days. She had decided to phone Miss Parry and ask whether she might move in earlier, when there was a tentative knock at the door.

She dried her eyes hastily and called, 'Come in.'

Mrs. Hardy peeped round the door, a cup and saucer in her hand. 'Brought you a nice cup of tea, dear.'

Selena sat up and attempted a smile. 'Thank you, Mrs. Hardy.'

Mrs. Hardy said uncertainly, 'It was the cufflink I found, wasn't it? Oh, Selena, have I messed things up for you?'

'It wasn't your fault.' Selena's voice roughened with tears again for a moment. 'He should have believed me.' Then she pulled herself together. 'I'm going to leave here as soon as possible.'

Mrs. Hardy withdrew, still murmuring confused apologies, and Selena drank her tea. Then she went to the bathroom and splashed her tear-stained face with cold water, tidied her hair, applied a little lipstick, and ran downstairs to the telephone.

Miss Parry was at home and said there would be no objection to Selena moving in the following morning.

Mrs. Hardy was hovering unhappily and Selena was surprised to see that it was almost noon. 'Isn't it time you were off, Mrs. Hardy?'

'I'm in no hurry. Shall I get you a bit of lunch?'

'I'm not hungry yet. You run along.'

'What are you going to do with yourself today? Why don't you go and see that nice Mr. Tremar?'

'I intend to,' Selena said grimly.

'That's right. Old friends are best, I always say.' She put on her coat. 'You won't forget to leave me your new address, will you?'

'Of course I won't. In any case, I'll see you tomorrow morning.'

★   ★   ★

At last she departed, and Selena began to pack up her last few belongings. They were mainly breakables, pictures and small pieces of china. There was already some form of wadding in the

193

bottom of the carton, so it took no time to wedge them in with old newspapers.

It was now two o'clock. Suddenly she could wait no longer to have a showdown with Stephen.

She put on a jacket and hurried down the lane, unaware of the spring sunshine or the song of the nesting birds. She was relieved to find Stephen alone in his drive, peering doubtfully into the bonnet of his car. His expression lightened when he saw her.

'Hello, Selena. Wretched thing's on its last legs, I'm afraid.' He made to kiss her, but she turned her face away.

'Can we talk, Stephen?'

'Of course.' He looked at her curiously. 'Do you want to go into the house?'

'Is Chris in?'

'Yes.'

'Can we go for a walk?'

His bewilderment deepened. He closed the car bonnet and wiped his hands on a rag. 'What's this about?'

She walked ahead of him down the

path, turning away from the village. Stephen hurried after her and caught at her arm. 'What is it, Selena?'

'Why didn't you tell me that you owned the land for the alternative road route?'

'What?' He stared at her. 'What did you say?'

'You heard what I said.'

His face flushed a dull red. 'Good grief, I never thought of it. I assumed you knew.'

'How could I know?'

'I probably forgot about it. It's belonged to the family since before I was born. What does it matter, anyway? The road will go by Cloudhallows. Any change was always a forlorn hope, particularly when Denning refused to come in with us.' He looked at her shrewdly. 'Is this his doing? Has he been prying into my concerns?'

'You tried your best to interest him in the affair. Can you blame him if he did his homework?'

'He's trying to come between us,

Selena. Can't you see that? He has done since the day he arrived.'

'No, he just didn't like being made to look a fool. Any more than I do. You could have told me of your real interest. You deceived all the village.'

'I wouldn't have got any support if it had been known that I had a special interest.' He tried to pull her into his arms. 'I did it for us, Selena. I wanted the money to put down on a decent house for us — '

She pulled away from him in distaste. 'Don't make me part of it. I didn't care what money you had, or didn't have. I've been poor in my time, goodness knows. In any case, I don't see how you can be as hard up as you're always complaining. I think you're just avaricious!'

She turned on her heel and strode off up the lane. Behind her she heard his furious tones. 'I suppose you're going to Denning? Mistress of Cloudhallows, just what you've always wanted. Will you put up with his other woman for that?'

Selena turned back to him. His face wore the sullen expression she realised now she had seen so often. She felt nothing but a slight regret. 'No, I don't expect to see Mark again. Or you, Stephen.'

★   ★   ★

She turned and walked away again, and this time he didn't follow her. She didn't feel like going home yet, but struck off across the fields above Cloudhallows.

So now all her bridges were burned. Michael, Mark, Stephen and Chrissie. How odd that it had been Stephen — who had always seemed so straightforward — and not Mark, who had resembled Michael in his devious dealings.

She walked for nearly an hour, not aware, until she was out of breath, of how fierce a pace she had been setting. She sat down, her back against a tree, and looked down over the quiet landscape until she was rested.

She took a gentler pace on her return to Cloudhallows. When she got back she prepared a meal for herself, then had a last check round and a final tidy up, before she retired to bed beneath its eaves for the last time.

The next morning she felt a little better at the prospect of action. She had bathed and breakfasted, and was loading her belongings in the boot of her car, when Mrs. Hardy arrived at nine o'clock.

'Oh, Selena, you're not going already? You weren't leaving without saying good-bye?'

'No, of course I wasn't, but I do want to make an early start.'

'Isn't Mr. Tremar going to help you move?'

'He'll be out on his rounds. In any case, it isn't necessary. I don't have anything heavy.'

She finished packing the boot to her satisfaction, then returned to the house for a while to talk with Mrs. Hardy, giving her a forwarding address and handing over her keys.

At last, after a tearful farewell, she was away. She took her time driving to Tivenham, not wanting to arrive too early, and was ringing Miss Parry's doorbell just after ten o'clock.

The elderly schoolteacher was delighted to see her and together they carried Selena's luggage into the hall, breaking for coffee before Selena carried it on up to the top floor.

The flat was attractive and welcoming with the morning sun streaming in. On a small table a jug of narcissus filled the air with heady fragrance. Selena unpacked her clothes and hung them up, and stowed away her suitcases. Delighted to see a large bookcase, she unpacked her books, but decided to postpone arranging them — a task she enjoyed too much to hurry — until she had been out to buy some food.

She picked up her shopping bag and ran downstairs, pausing at the kitchen to ask Miss Parry's advice about local shops. Miss Parry gave her instructions, inviting her to lunch when she returned.

Selena found the well-stocked corner shop and bought some groceries, adding a bottle of wine to which she hoped Miss Parry would not object.

Far from objecting, Miss Parry was delighted, and the two women enjoyed a companionable lunch that lasted until well into the afternoon, as Miss Parry brought Selena up to date with news of early schoolfriends.

At last Selena got back to her own flat. She passed a pleasant hour arranging her books, then turned to the last remaining carton. This contained her china and other breakables, and she unwrapped them carefully.

* * *

When the contents were safely on the table, she screwed up the newspaper and stuffed it back in the box, ready for disposal with the rest of her empties. As she did so, she noticed the material wedged in the bottom of the carton. It looked in good condition and she wondered if it had been left there accidentally. She rummaged among the newspaper and drew it out. Her heart sank. It was Chrissie's red anorak, a fairly new acquisition. She was going to have to return the wretched thing.

She held the garment against her, attempting to smooth out the creases, and her heart gave a sudden lurch. Right across the front of the anorak, just above the waist, was a faint line of primrose paint.

Selena's mouth went dry. She remembered the last time she had seen the anorak. Chrissie had been wearing it when she had called on Selena the previous Saturday afternoon, when she had brought her uncharacteristic gift of flowers.

She never left the house. The solution hit her like a blow. Nobody had needed a key. When Chris had apparently left by the back door, she had simply concealed herself in the coat cupboard until Selena had left.

Then she had turned off the heating and opened the windows, getting the still-damp paint from the sills on her coat as she pushed at them. After that she had merely to drop the door-catch behind her.

'I knew there was something odd about that visit,' Selena thought. 'She had no dogs with her.' When was Chris ever out on foot without at least one dog?

Sick and shaken, she retreated to her room and sat down on the bed. Had Stephen been involved in the scheme? she wondered. Was he, in fact, the instigator? Somehow she thought not. He had been quite at ease when she had arrived at his house, and throughout the evening in her company.

She had never seriously suspected Chris. After all, Selena's growing involvement with Mark should have steered her away from Stephen. But, she now realised, Chris had no inkling of that involvement. Selena had done her best to conceal it. It was true that

Chris had teased her a little about Mark but, infatuated as she was herself, she was incapable of believing that anyone might prefer another man to her cousin. She was afraid of Stephen being taken away from her. The humiliation of being excluded from their evening meal had fuelled her feelings and she was prepared to do anything to get rid of Selena or, at least, to hit out at her.

Now, she supposed, she would have to return the anorak, have a showdown with Chris, and apologise to Mark — and Fiona. But not yet. Much as she longed to have done with this chapter of her life, she couldn't face another confrontation yet. For the present, she would return Chris' jacket without comment and let Chris explain it to Stephen if she cared to.

★ ★ ★

She made herself a cup of tea with the electric kettle Miss Parry had thoughtfully provided, then wrapped the anorak up in brown paper. She went out to her car and set out for Fairbridge. She had hoped not to have to return to the village and was glad that it was almost dusk when she parked in the shadows of the Tremars' hedge. There was no one about as she opened the gate and tiptoed up the path to deposit the package in the porch.

She returned to her car, engaged the clutch as quietly as possible, and drove away. As she neared the Corner House and the turn for Cloudhallows, her attention was caught by the tall chimneys of the house, visible over the trees. A thin thread of smoke curled up from them.

Before she realised what she was doing she had made a hasty turn into the lane and braked. Someone was in residence, presumably Mark. Should she go now and make her apologies, before she had time to lose her nerve? She yearned to have the whole business over and done with. She needn't go in. She *must not* go in. Just a brief dignified explanation, then a retreat to her new refuge.

She released the brake and slowly ascended the lane. As she passed the gate, she saw Mark's car parked on the foundations for the new garage. She parked in the lay-by and walked back to the house. Her heart was thumping against her ribs and her legs were shaking, but she forced herself on.

She reached the front door and pushed the bell before she had time to change her mind. Immediately she wished that she had given herself time to compose some sort of reasonably articulate opening. There was no response to the bell and she rang a second time. She wondered why he didn't answer the door. She could hear neither TV or music within, and he was unlikely to have gone for a walk in the chilly dusk. She had rung for the third time, and was turning away, when she heard footsteps approaching the door. She steeled herself as the bolt was undone.

Then the door opened and Fiona stood on the threshold. She wore a negligee, inadequately clutched around her and, on her face, such a look of mixed irritation, happiness, and naked fulfilment, that it tore at Selena's heart.

7

'Oh, Da-arling!' Fiona drawled. 'Very bad timing!' Selena stood dumbstruck. The reason for her call had totally deserted her.

'Well?' Fiona queried impatiently. 'What is it you want? You'll understand if I don't ask you in?'

Selena would have died sooner than enter the house. She heard herself saying, 'It doesn't matter. It isn't important.' And then she was blundering down the path, tears blinding her eyes.

She got back to her car and hunched over the wheel, struggling to regain her composure, but great sobs racked her body.

How could he? her outraged heart protested. 'We were together in that house only yesterday.' And how breathtakingly hypocritical of him to be angry over her supposed infidelity. Or had that just been an act? she wondered miserably — a quick reaction to an opportunity to get himself off the hook over a situation that had gone too far?

Oh, he and Fiona suited each other very well, as he had almost spelled out to her. No nonsense there about trust or commitment. She had a sudden vision of them now, sophisticated and worldly, laughing together at her inopportune appearance, perhaps even watching her from the bedroom window.

The thought gave her a sickening jolt. She scrubbed hard at her eyes, tilted her chin, started the engine, and set off back to Tivenham.

How right she had been, she told herself. How very sensible to get out when she had. But sobs still shook her, the lump in her throat was agonising, and tears kept filling her eyes and had to be firmly squeezed away in order to see her way clearly.

Somehow she got back to Tivenham.

She parked the car and tiptoed upstairs, fearful of rousing Miss Parry. Once in her room, she undressed and put on her dressing-gown. It had been a long and eventful day, but she knew sleep was out of the question. She made herself a cup of tea and drank it, staring unseeingly ahead, her eyes hot, dry and painful.

$$\star \quad \star \quad \star$$

Three days later, in the early afternoon, Mark let himself into Cloudhallows. As he looked around the hall, he frowned slightly. There was a thin layer of dust on all the surfaces and dead flowers in the vases. Mrs. Hardy, who might have been persuaded to stay on, had been antagonised by Fiona and taken herself off.

Well, it probably wouldn't be difficult to replace her. But Selena, that was a different matter. Selena was the very heart and spirit of the house.

He sighed heavily. How could he

have been so wrong over anybody? But he had been wrong before, and to go open-eyed into a relationship that could mean a repeat of the misery of his first marriage was something he wasn't prepared to do.

He flung open some windows to air the house, then carried the two vases of dead flowers through to the kitchen and emptied them, rinsing out the vases. Fiona had left the remains of a meal on the kitchen table and he put those dishes in the sink to soak.

The two sturdy stoneware mugs from which he had drunk coffee with Selena stood on the draining-board and he picked one up, turning it in his hands. She had certainly got to him. He was behaving like a sentimental schoolboy. Why could he no longer rouse any fury in himself at the thought of her plottings with Stephen Tremar?

He put down the mug and went upstairs to see what signs of occupancy Fiona had left there. A discreet little lovenest, she had called it, suddenly realising its potential.

He had felt distaste at her using the house for her purpose, but he could not have explained it to her. He couldn't bear the thought that she had used Selena's room, but Selena's room was a modest one and, needless to say, Fiona had used the main bedroom.

He tidied up the mess in the big bedroom, then looked into Selena's room. It was pin-neat and her faint perfume, not quite drowned by Fiona's more strident one, reminded him painfully of her presence. Then he remembered that she had been here with another man. It was merely that she was more discreet than Fiona.

He sat down on the bed and buried his head in his hands. A wave of longing and loss engulfed him. He was almost ready to seek her out and plead with her to come to him on any terms.

There was a sudden loud knock at the front door and he pulled himself together and went downstairs, praying that it might be Selena.

A strikingly handsome man that he had never seen before stood on the doorstep.

At Mark's look of enquiry the stranger said easily, 'Hello! You'll be the new owner, I guess?'

'That's right.'

'Very nice place you have. The point is, old man, I spent a night here a few days ago and somehow I managed to mislay a cufflink — ' He stopped, realising that Mark was staring at him with a curious expression.

After a second, Mark said curtly, 'It was found. I'll fetch it.' He turned to go inside and Michael followed, uninvited, at his heels.

★ ★ ★

Mark retrieved the cufflink from the saucer on the kitchen dresser where it had reposed since it had been found. Fighting an urge to pummel the debonair smiling face, he said in the same strangled voice, 'It has a sentimental

212

value, I imagine.'

'Oh, no, nothing like that.' Michael accepted the link, tossing it lightly in his hand. 'But I'm afraid they'll have to pay another visit to uncle soon.'

'Uncle?'

'Yes. To be frank, I was trying to raise a little capital when I called here, but my ex-wife seems finally to have had enough of me. Slung me out into the night. Well, into the morning, actually. A chaste couch and a sandwich was all that I got from her — '

A great flood of relief swept over Mark, leaving him weak. He said, 'You're Michael?'

'That's me. Do you know Selena?'

'We — overlapped.'

'A great girl. I led her the devil of a life but, sad to say, I'm afraid she has grown up at last.'

'Well — it's nice to meet you.' Mark was beaming at him. 'Would you like a drink?'

Michael wondered for a brief moment whether there was anything that might be extracted from this man who had inexplicably turned so benevolent, then he said reluctantly, 'No, thanks, I'd better be getting along. I've just borrowed a friend's car for an hour.'

The two men said goodbye warmly and Mark turned back into the house. His heart was near to bursting with joy and relief. He must find Selena and beg her to forgive him. His old mistrust of another woman was a poor excuse, but all he had. Selena, he was sure, would understand.

His eye lighted on the little desk in the study. Selena had once said that she would like it, and the cabinet in her bedroom. His cheque was with the estate, they were now his property. He would take them to Selena and ask her to accept them. And to accept him, too? He scarcely dared hope.

★   ★   ★

The three days that Selena had spent in Tivenham were among the worst of her life. She went through them like a zombie, feeling drugged and empty, yet unable to eat or sleep. She tried to avoid contact with Miss Parry. She could see that her old friend was anxious about her and she dreaded any questioning.

It was teatime on the third day and she was wondering how she could face another endless evening, when Miss Parry called up to her that she had a visitor.

Selena leaned over the bannister and saw Mark below in the hall. Already pale, her face went ashen and she swayed, so that Mark quickly ran up the stairs. On the upper landing he stopped at arms length from her, sensing the barrier between them.

'Are you all right?' he said.

Selena gripped the bannister tightly in an effort to control her faintness.

'Yes, I'm fine. What do you want?'

'I brought the cabinet and the desk that you wanted. I managed to get them in the car — ' His voice trailed away.

The words sounded so inadequate.

For a moment Selena couldn't understand what he was talking about, then she said, 'Oh, yes. I'd forgotten about them. Thank you. I'll give you a cheque.'

'I don't want any money. Shall I bring them up?'

'Thank you,' Selena said again. She had to get rid of him if only for a minute. He went back downstairs and she returned to her room, sitting down abruptly in the armchair before her legs jack-knifed beneath her. In the mirror above the mantelshelf she saw her pale distraught face reflected. She pressed her hands together to stop them trembling. 'Let me be cool and self-possessed,' she prayed. 'Don't let me show him that I care.'

She heard Mark make his two journeys up and down the stairs, then he tapped lightly on her door and carried first the cabinet and then the desk into her room.

'Where do you want them?'

'Oh — anywhere. I'll arrange them.

Thank you for bringing them.' She waited, but he showed no signs of leaving. The civilised thing would be to offer him a cup of coffee, but she couldn't do it. She said, 'How did you find me?'

'I called on Mrs. Hardy and asked her where you had gone. She was very severe with me, but I persuaded her that I wanted to apologise.'

'Apologise?'

'For upsetting you last Wednesday morning. For my filthy accusations. It was unforgivable after — after what had happened between us. My only excuse is that my trust has been betrayed many times before. But not by you. It was inexcusable.'

Selena looked at him as though barely understanding what he was saying. Why should he make such a point of apologising for his behaviour on Wednesday when the very next day he had been with Fiona? Was this all part of a cruel and elaborate joke between them?

Mark had half-turned away before her stricken face. 'Well — I can't expect you to understand — '

'I understand. It doesn't matter.'

'It matters to me! Your ex-husband called and explained that the cufflink belonged to him.'

★   ★   ★

To tidy up the loose ends, although it seemed so trivial now, Selena said, 'I have to say sorry, too. About the windows. I didn't open them, but I have discovered who did and, in a way, I *was* responsible. I called at Cloudhallows, but Fiona — ' The pain and embarrassment of that encounter flooded back and Selena turned her head away.

'I didn't get your message, but I haven't seen Fiona since Monday.'

Very slowly what he had said penetrated Selena's numbed mind. She repeated, 'You haven't seen Fiona since Monday?'

'That's right. She's taking a few days off.'

'But your car was outside Cloud-hallows when I called on Thursday evening.'

'I lent it to Fiona. I'm using one from the pool. It's all supposed to be very hush-hush, but she has a new boy friend. He's something of a VIP. She's probably exaggerating wildly, as she's inclined to do but, according to her, governments — if not quite toppling — would teeter a little if their affair was discovered. She felt that her own car was too noticeable, and to use her friend's car would be indiscreet.'

Misreading Selena's stunned expression, he added, 'I did say she tends to over-dramatise.'

Selena whispered, 'I thought you were with her.'

'No, I see quite enough of Fiona during the day! Maybe I shouldn't condone this affair, but I owe a lot to her. That's why, as I'm sure you've noticed, I let her have a lot of her own way. She's a spoilt brat, but she does have her good points. But I didn't come here to talk about Fiona. I wanted to apologise for being such a brute to you after — after what was the sweetest night of my life.' He turned towards the door. 'I'll go now.'

'Mark, you don't understand. I thought you were with her.'

He turned back. She was on her feet, her face alight with hope.

'You thought Fiona and I?'

She nodded. Tears welled up into her eyes and tumbled on to her cheeks. 'Someone was there with her. They had been making love. I thought it was you.'

'Oh, my darling!' He pulled her roughly into his arms. 'How could you think that?'

'I thought you were so well suited,' Selena murmured into his neck. 'You said you didn't want to get too involved. You said you only wanted a mutually enjoyable relationship between people who know the rules of the game.' She tried to laugh.

'And so I did in theory, but, unfortunately, it doesn't work for me.' He put his hand beneath her chin and tilted her tear-stained face up to meet his. He looked into her swimming eyes. 'Since I met you, nothing else will do for me.'

Very gently he kissed her on her lips, her eyes, her face. Then he returned to her mouth and his long slow kisses grew in passion as he pulled her pliant body closer and closer to him.

After a long time he broke off to say, a little breathlessly, 'Selena, my love, say that you'll marry me!'

'I'll marry you!' Selena responded.

'Shall we live at Cloudhallows?'

'It's too big for us,' she protested.

'It may not always be too big . . . '

'The trunk road will soon run past it.'

'I'd live on the runway of Concorde with you.' He frowned. 'Ungrateful wench! Why the sudden reluctance? I thought you were crazy about the place.'

Selena kissed him in a manner in which reluctance had no part. 'I just wanted you to be quite, quite sure that I wasn't marrying you for Cloud-hallows!'

THE END

We do hope that you have enjoyed reading this large print book.

Did you know that all of our titles are available for purchase?

We publish a wide range of high quality large print books including:
**Romances, Mysteries, Classics
General Fiction
Non Fiction and Westerns**

Special interest titles available in large print are:
**The Little Oxford Dictionary
Music Book, Song Book
Hymn Book, Service Book**

Also available from us courtesy of Oxford University Press:
**Young Readers' Dictionary
(large print edition)
Young Readers' Thesaurus
(large print edition)**

For further information or a free brochure, please contact us at:
**Ulverscroft Large Print Books Ltd.,
The Green, Bradgate Road, Anstey,
Leicester, LE7 7FU, England.
Tel:** (00 44) **0116 236 4325
Fax:** (00 44) **0116 234 0205**

THE WAYWARD HEART

Stella Kent

Francesca had loved her unruffled way of life, working in the Lynford bookshop with fatherly Mr. Pinkerton. But it had all come to an abrupt end when the shop was sold over Mr. Pinkerton's head, by his nephew Adam. The news caused the old man's death, and fury overwhelmed Francesca. But when Adam offered her a job in the Paris bookshop, she accepted. Here was a chance to get all she could out of a particularly heartless man . . .

A KISS AND A PROMISE

Moyra Tarling

Just as Autumn Daniels is getting her life back together after her husband's death, Matt Kingston returns. He'd left her five years ago with a kiss and a promise he never kept. Then, pregnant and alone, she'd turned to his brother — however, his proposal of marriage was just an elaborate scheme of vengeance. But now, as Matt melts the ice around her heart, is it Autumn he wants — or his daughter? This time, is his promise of love forever?

TOMORROW'S PROMISE

Gillian Villiers

Lara is determined never to risk falling in love, but when she takes up a new teaching post, finds it isn't quite so simple. She shares a house with fellow teacher Mick, whose laid-back manner hides a warm heart that threatens to melt even Lara's cool exterior. Trying to distract herself with a spot of property development only seems to involve her in endless problems, which Mick is more than happy to help resolve. But should she let him?